ALSO BY LYNN FREED

THE LAST LAUGH

LYNN FREED

The LAST LAUGH

a novel

SARAH CRICHTON BOOKS
Farrar, Straus and Giroux ı New York

Sarah Crichton Books
Farrar, Straus and Giroux
18 West 18th Street, New York 10011

Printed in the United States of America
First edition, 2017

Library of Congress Cataloging-in-Publication Data
Names: Freed, Lynn, author.
Title: The last laugh : a novel / Lynn Freed.
Description: First edition. | New York : Sarah Crichton Books/
    Farrar, Straus and Giroux, 2017.
Identifiers: LCCN 2016052196 | ISBN 9780374286651
    (hardcover) | ISBN 9780374713676 (ebook)
Subjects: LCSH: Female friendship—Fiction. | Older
    women—Fiction. | BISAC: FICTION / Literary. |
    FICTION / Contemporary Women. | FICTION / Family
    Life.
Classification: LCC PR9369.3.F68 L37 2017 |
    DDC 823/.914—dc23
LC record available at https://lccn.loc.gov/2016052196

Designed by Richard Oriolo

Our books may be purchased in bulk for promotional,
educational, or business use. Please contact your local
bookseller or the Macmillan Corporate and Premium Sales
Department at 1-800-221-7945, extension 5442, or by e-mail at
MacmillanSpecialMarkets@macmillan.com.

www.fsgbooks.com
www.twitter.com/fsgbooks
www.facebook.com/fsgbooks

10 9 8 7 6 5 4 3 2 1

For RWK

All I want to do is go on with the unbridled life I lead here: barefoot, my faded bathing suit, an old jacket, lots of garlic, and swimming at all hours of the day.

—COLETTE, AT SIXTY

DRAMATIS PERSONAE

AGNES: forty-three, daughter of Bess, mother of two, lives in
California, life coach, British and American

AMOS: Dania's late husband, Israeli American

BESS: sixty-nine, half sister of Ruth, born and grew up in
South Africa, lived in London for almost forty years, recently
moved from there to California, has a bouquet of passports

CLIVE: seventy-five, Ruth's ex-husband, a doctor, naturalized
American

DANIA: sixty-nine, psychotherapist, born and grew up in Israel,
lives in California

DIONYSOS: sixtyish, Bess's taxi driver and general factotum,
retired ship's engineer, Greek

ELEFTHERIA: about forty-five, Greek cleaning woman

EMMA: nine, daughter of Agnes

FINN: seventy-two, Ruth's sometime American lover, lives in California

GILES: six, son of Agnes

GLADNESS: sixty-nine, Bess's childhood friend, now companion, Zulu

HESTER: forty-two, daughter of Ruth and Hugh, born in South Africa, grew up in London, moved to California with Ruth when she was fifteen, lecturer in sociology

HUGH: Ruth's late South African lover, father of Hester, murdered in South Africa before Hester was born, sugar magnate

IRINA: about eighteen, au pair for Mohammed, Moldovan

LILY: sixteen, Hester's daughter, American

MOHAMMED: fourteen months, adopted child of Wilfred and Tarquin, British

NOAM: thirty-five, Dania's son, lives in Albany, New York, a teacher

PATIENCE: forty-eight, daughter of Gladness, lives in South Africa, Zulu

REX: sixtyish, Bess's sometime lover, lives wherever he can, British

RUTH: sixty-nine, born in South Africa, lives in California, bestselling writer of detective fiction

TARQUIN: thirty, husband of Wilfred, British

WENDY: about fifty-five, patient of Dania, American

WILFRED: forty, son of Bess, lives in London, dermatologist, British

YAEL: forty-one, daughter of Dania, lives in California, research scientist, American

THE LAST LAUGH

WE'D PUT PASSION BEHIND US, we said, I more loudly than the others. Not that men had lost their charm, we said, not really. It was just that the blinders were gone, the sport, the spring and sway of the dance, the careless unreasoning madness of it all. Anyway, we said, passion had accomplished its chief work, at least from a biological point of view—children and grandchildren. What we wanted now was peace. Ourselves to ourselves. No service, no duty, no motherly or grandmotherly obligations.

If we'd kept all this to ourselves—if we hadn't run amok with the idea of freedom and escape—we'd probably have got away with far less trouble. But, of course, we didn't keep things to ourselves; we were enjoying the effect too much, even on our children. They were astounded. Then resentful. Our passion, they'd assumed, now lay with them, now that they were parents themselves—they'd reeled us in at last. And even if, from time to time, they suspected we might prefer our time to ourselves, they'd never imagined it would come to this. Can you believe them? they asked each other. Can you believe what those mad old bags are up to?

Well, here we were now, three mad old bags and a bottle of ouzo out on our stone terrace, the sun setting far below over the Aegean.

"Gott!" said Dania. "Why did we wait so long?"

She was always asking this, always answering herself, as well. "We had to grow up ourselves," she would say.

But growing up wasn't the point; money was. Without it, without what we'd accumulated over the years one way or another, none of us would have been able to budge, certainly not to an island far enough away to make spontaneous visits by the children unlikely.

The island had been my idea. I'd come here on a sort of honeymoon with Clive and had known even then that I would return one day without him. So now here I was, almost fifty years on, and it was just as I'd left it—heat, sea, salt air, octopuses strung out along a line at the port, and, up here, the white houses, blue doors, beaded curtains, cobbled streets, the bougainvillea and church bells, and the fishmonger's cry every morning.

Bess kicked out her plump tanned legs. "Grow up?" she said. "What the hell for?"

I'd brought her into the arrangement when Flora, our natural third, got cold feet. Bess was a new friend—more than a friend, as she'd been quick to inform me. Her mother, she said, had had an affair with my father, and her grandmother with my mother's father, and so we were half sisters in one way and God knows what in the other, and all this I'd only found out when she'd phoned out of the blue about a year before to say she was now in California, living with her daughter, and didn't I remember her from South Africa? Didn't I remember when her grandmother once brought her to our house for tea?

Well, no, I didn't, not at first anyway. But then, yes, I thought I did remember a bold, plump girl emptying her tea into her saucer, and my mother, straight and stiff and silent, watching her wipe her mouth across her sleeve.

I smiled out into the fading light. For six weeks things had been going smoothly. This we put down to the guidelines we'd all agreed on before we left. Sooner or later, we'd said, the children would get over their resentment and start coming to visit, and did we want to be running a B&B? With a nursery school attached? Okay, we'd said, here's what we'll do: pool some money and rent the house down the hill for the month of June. Then they'll just have to work out some sort of time-share arrangement among themselves. On condition they understand that up here there'll be no cooking, no babysitting either. What about that?

Wonderful! we said. Excellent! All the wheedling and pleading out of earshot, and, oh God, the threats never carried out, the time-outs and squatting to reason eye to eye when one good smack on the bum could bring it to an end. They're terrified of their children, we decided, appeasing them like little household gods. Perhaps they consider it insurance against being consigned to an ice floe when their own time comes, we said—well, ha ha to that!

"And anyway," I said, kicking off my shoes, "here we are. And none of us, not even Dania, is suffering a moment's guilt."

"Guilt!" cried Bess. "What the hell for?"

She had a point, although all our lives Dania and I had subordinated husbands, children, lovers to our careers. We'd met when our first books came out—mine a detective novel, and hers a treatise on the psycho-social efficacies of infidelity. Bess, on the other hand, had made a career out of lovers, taking off for months at a time, leaving her children to Gladness.

Gladness was another matter. She was the daughter of one of the Zulu maids in Bess's grandmother's hotel, where she and Bess had grown up together. Once Bess was married and living in London, it was Gladness she'd really missed—Gladness her grandmother had sent over to be with her when Agnes was born.

So now she wanted Gladness here, with us. She wouldn't interfere, she assured us, we could find a room for her in the village, what was wrong with that? The thing was, she said, Gladdy was lost without her—they were lost without each other. And Dania should just get over her squeamishness; she wasn't living on a kibbutz anymore.

Dania lifted her eyebrows at me.

But the truth was I didn't want Gladness either. Bess and I might both have grown up in South Africa, but that was then, and now, in this life, even Eleftheria coming in to clean and sweep every morning felt like an intrusion. The thought of Gladness hauling herself up the hill every day, the Greeks eyeing her as if she were going to run off with their washing—well, no!

"*She's* the one I feel guilty about," said Bess, "not Agnes or Wilfred. She's devoted her life to me."

"Look it," Dania said in the low, measured voice she used on her patients, "what if she spends here a visit with the children?

In June? Help them with the little ones, maybe?" She gave her therapeutic smile.

"But that's the problem," Bess wailed. "She's too old to be a nanny now! And, anyway, she's a bigot."

Dania glanced at me. *You understand what's going on here?* "She's bigoted about Greeks?" she asked calmly.

"No!" cried Bess. "About blacks."

"*Blecks?*"

"Wilfred's child—the one they just adopted—he's black. That's why she wants to move out."

"Gott!" The glance again. "And what about Wilfred? She doesn't object to a homosexual?"

"No!" said Bess miserably. "She was his nanny. You don't understand! If there's anyone I feel guilty about, it's *her*! She hates London! She's always hated it! And now this!"

I rarely suffered guilt myself but, when I did, I thought I understood its deep stab of regret. "Wouldn't she prefer to go back to South Africa?" I suggested. "Doesn't she have a daughter there?"

"She wouldn't prefer that at all!" cried Bess. "She's dead scared in that country now, everyone just waiting for a chance to rob and murder you. Patience has no time for her unless she wants money, and the grandson's in and out of jail. So, don't you see? Gladdy's home is with *me*, wherever *I* happen to be. And that's here, now, with us."

She shifted her chair away from us, into the last beam of sun. All her life, it seemed, she'd been used to getting her own way, and if she couldn't, she sulked. When neither Dania nor I took any notice of the sulking, she was left a bit bewildered without its power.

Looking at her there, it occurred to me that a woman in her

late sixties who behaved like a child might be more of a problem than any child itself.

☙

I'D KNOWN FROM THE BEGINNING, of course, that we'd be getting on each other's nerves from time to time. We'd all known this. So, despite the fact that we were all talkers—because of it, really—we'd decided in advance to try to contend with such irritations in silence. Talking things through, the current fashion, only served to produce resentment and anger, I suggested. And even Dania—who, after all, made a living listening to people talking things through—had to agree.

But then there I was the next morning, biting back my irritation not only with Bess, who, once again, had consumed all the baklava in the middle of the night—leaving the tin on the table for the ants to find—but also with Dania and her relentless boasting. Over the years I'd tried everything I could think of to get her to give it up. Just the night before I had talked about the boaster and name-dropper I'd once suffered at an artists' colony. "He was a room clearer," I'd said. "People vied not to sit at his table."

"Oy! Oy!" Dania cried. "Name-droppers!"

"But also boasters," I said. "They go together."

"Of course!" she said knowingly. "Of course!"

So it was hopeless. And now here she was again, breakfast over and me excusing myself to go off and write my column, saying, "Look it, Ruthi! I've got sixteen books and ninety-two articles"—she was still including translations although I'd told her time and again that they didn't count—"so why I should write any more? Ruthi! It's time here to relax!"

Bess watched us in silence. In a moment of exasperation, I'd made the mistake of confiding to her my irritation with Dania's boasting. I adore her, of course, I'd said, but—

And she hadn't leapt in. Bess could be surprising in this way—unjealous, untricky. Anyway, she was far more concerned about Dania's peasant skirts and gypsy jewelry. She seemed to consider bad dress a character flaw closely associated with higher education. I, who was just as highly educated, had somehow been spared, said she, probably because I didn't hold the education as dear. And, meanwhile, couldn't we at least entice Dania away from that ghastly musk perfume she was so devoted to? What about giving her the bottle of Chanel No. 5 Bess had bought at duty-free?

Bess herself was devoted to high fashion and had given up on formal education the day she left school. Every week she summoned Dionysos, the taxi driver, to take her down to the port for her manicure, and every two weeks for a pedicure that involved a tank of small flesh-eating fish. She also checked impatiently at the post office for her copies of *Harper's Bazaar* and *Vogue*, both the U.S. and U.K. editions. When one finally came in, she'd hurry back up to the house, lay her bulk out along the window seat, glasses down her nose, and be deaf to whatever was going on around her. Once she had scoured the magazine, she'd move on to fashion sites on the Internet, clicking, ordering, canceling, looking up to say, "There's a perfect swing jacket at forty percent off here for you, Ruth. Greeny beige. Very you."

Once, she had been quite a beauty, that was clear from her photos—an olive-skinned, black-haired beauty with wide, dark eyes and an ironic twist to the mouth. In fact, she was not unlike my father—*our* father, I kept reminding myself—the skin, the nose, and her face was still unlined at sixty-nine thanks to the fat and the face-lifts. Strolling past the weathered island women with their buns and hairy moles and little mustaches, she looked almost youthful in her white linen tents and ballet flats, her smooth skin oiled and gleaming.

I was the only one of us who hadn't had a face-lift, although Dania claimed that vanity had had nothing to do with hers. "I had to push back my head to see," she said. "I was looking at everything through slots."

She meant "slits," of course, but I'd learned over the years not to correct her English—she didn't take it well. Anyway, it was too divinely wrong to bear straightening out. "Scrap the bottom of the barrel," "pied-à-tête," "skin thin." She spoke the way she drove and sang and cooked—with a disdain for details others might consider necessary, but which she managed quite well without, thank you. She'd driven tanks in the Israeli army, sung and danced and cooked and written her sixteen books and ninety-two articles, and, See? she would say, emerging from the kitchen triumphant. Who needs all that fuss with live tomatoes? I did it with cans!

"I'll just do this column," I said, "and then I'll be able to relax."

"Three hundred words, Ruthi? You'll come through it as usual with flowing colors!"

The column was my fault. I'd suggested the idea to the new features editor at *So Long Magazine* as a sort of lark—a diary of our year, I'd said, never imagining they'd want it weekly, or that they'd call it "Granny à Go Go." So now, week to week the deadline haunted me. No sooner did I finish one column than I was worrying about the next. And the worst of it was that I was supposed to leave out everything that wasn't "à go go." How, after all, could I write about the boasting or the baklava? Or Hester's voice on the phone, tight with resentment, the knot that formed under my ribs as I tried in vain to warm her back to me? Or even Gladness? Especially Gladness? How could I write about a beloved old Zulu nanny for an audience rich in embracers of good conscience?

Well, I couldn't. I wasn't writer enough for the task. Or woman enough. I wanted my daughter's blessing and my friends' love. And if they got on my nerves, the lot of them, I seemed to count on not getting on theirs. So, it was hopeless—all that bravado in leaving, and now this: boasters and bingers and a deadline that hung like a stone around my neck. The whole thing was a luxury, I decided, all of it, even my discontent, which, doubtless, would be gone by tomorrow.

I closed the door to my room and opened the laptop.

☙

à gg, Greece

My favorite time of day for a drive down to town is the evening, the sun setting over the bay and the last of the ferries unloading its passengers. Winding down past ancient olive trees, I remember to add olives to my grocery list. And feta. The farmers who come to the port to sell their wares will be gone by now, but the local shops will be opening for the evening and I'm thinking of trotting past the ceramicist to see whether he's lowered the price on the octopus platter I've been eyeing for my daughter—

☙

I PUSHED ON, PUSHING THE piece up the hill again and into the kitchen for the sort of evening meal we never actually cooked—marinated lamb on the spit, roast potatoes with rosemary, Greek salad. Bess couldn't cook, Dania knew only cans and casseroles, and I was damned if I'd land up in an apron night after night.

Recipe for marinade
1 cup olive oil
1 cup full-bodied red wine

6 cloves of garlic, peeled and sliced
1 sprig of fresh rosemary
1 bay leaf
salt and black pepper, to taste

☙

I SENT IT OFF, AND then pulled out the gorgeous marbled note-book I'd bought in Florence years ago. The thought had been to begin a journal, forgetting, as I stood in the shop turning the thing in my hands, that I wasn't a natural journal keeper. And now, every time I opened it, there seemed nothing I could say that would warrant marring the thick creamy paper. Anyway, for whom would I be writing it? Myself? That seemed a silly, self-conscious thing to do. Not to mention grandiose. And, in some way I couldn't define, illegitimate.

And yet I was sorry now that I didn't have a record of the past, if only to look back on the gripes and miseries and triumphs, to see how small they might seem at a distance. Or, perhaps, to render them small by putting them into words. I didn't know, really. It could be like looking through old photo albums, which I did quite often, the photos losing their life the more familiar they became.

And then, one day, Dania suggested that writing down the difficulties I'd had with Hester over the years might help put them into manageable shape. Particularly here, at such a remove. It would be like laying a ghost, she seemed to be saying, although God knows how she'd have mangled that metaphor if she'd got hold of it.

I unscrewed my pen and wrote "Hester #1" on the first page, underlining it, marring the book for good.

☙

Hester #1

In the time since I'd brought Hester from London to America, she'd turned from a plump, pink, earnest English schoolgirl to a sarcastic hulking American, flinging blame at me for all the unearned misery of her adolescence. There she stood at the top of the stairs in her Lanz nightie, her mouth twisted in fury. "I knew you'd forget the book!" she screamed. "That's so typical!"

The book I'd forgotten to pick up at the bookstore was for a report she had to write during our Mexican holiday. What was really enraging her, however, was not the book but the new man in my life—the lightness he'd brought me, the dinner we'd just had, and from which I'd returned very reluctantly because the next morning she and I were to catch an early plane to Puerto Vallarta.

I looked at my watch. "Jump into something," I said. "They close in twelve minutes. We'll race down there and you'll dash in and pick it up."

None of the girls in her class had invited her to go off with them for spring break. Why should they have? She had none of the lightness that American teenagers affected. She tried to bluster her way into their company with boasts about the father she'd never known, about London, even about me and my books.

"You're the one who forgot!" she shouted. "You go and get it!"

And so began yet another of our fights. They seemed to be visiting us more and more often these days—quick, shrieking, towering fights, with insults hurled, deep, cutting, irretrievable insults.

I walked past her and into my room. "With that attitude, you can forget about Mexico," I said. "I'll just cancel the tickets."

"I'll go anyway!" she shouted back, just as furious. "It's my money. My father left it for me, not you!"

Which is when, in the sort of access of power that has people running out of burning buildings with grand pianos on their backs, I stormed into her room, grabbed her passport, and tore it end to end.

Even now, considering that night, and the awful week at Club Med that followed, I wonder why I didn't tear her in half, or at least that ghastly flannel nightie. I wonder, too, at the role she has chosen for me, now that she is middle-aged, and at the way I tend to speak its lines as if they were my own, so that when, like tonight, I sense myself failing in the role, it feels like failing at being myself.

◉

DANIA WAS THE FIRST TO notice that Bess was up to something with Dionysos, the taxi driver. For some weeks, she'd been late returning from her run to the port, and now she was staying in town for a concert in the square. Not to worry, she said, he'd drop her home afterward.

"I'm telling you," said Dania, "it's that taxi driver, never mind he's so short and fet."

When he came for Bess, he'd leave his car at the entrance to the village, and then walk to the house, waiting in the hall, just out of the sun. After they'd left, we'd open the door to the veranda to air out his cologne. "Whew!" I'd say. "Dear God! What is it?"

Bess had never learned to drive. "What for?" she said. She'd only be a danger on the road. Anyway, driving in London was madness. And driving in Greece was worse.

Still, she insisted on contributing equally to the rental of our car. That was the agreement, she said, and it wasn't our fault that she was handicapped for normal living, just as she didn't expect us to drive her down to the port because she happened to be addicted to urban life.

So now she had Dionysos to drive her, and what if there was a wife somewhere? Dania said. A violent Greek wife? By the sound of it, Bess herself hadn't been far off a violent Greek wife when she'd caught Rex, her last lover, with Wilfred's au pair. And even if, as Bess said, it wasn't so much the dalliance as the yacht he'd chartered with her money to sail the girl around the Mediterranean—and this after the fortune he'd lost her through his harebrained schemes, reducing her from a house in St. John's Wood to a rented dump in Camden Town—well, thank God she still had the small inheritance our grandfather had left to her mother. Which, she was always quick to add, I should consider ours, since he'd left nothing to my mother, his legitimate daughter.

"You think she goes to bed with him?" Dania said. We were sitting out on the veranda in a cloud of mosquito repellent now, a boom box throbbing down the hill. "Oy! Oy, Ruthi! Can you imagine it? With that taxi driver?"

For all her years on a kibbutz, Dania was a snob. Never mind class or money, it was education that counted for her, professional success, standing in the world.

"Male attention can be a powerful aphrodisiac," I said, realizing as I did that, at least for my part, there also needed to be male laughter. And how much, suddenly, I missed it.

"Yes, yes, but with that *taxi driver!*"

"Bess is a sensualist."

"You said it! The chocolates, the baklava—"

And on we went, cozying back into our old friendship. Perhaps, I thought, Dania had been feeling left out over the past couple of months in the face of the common ground I shared with Bess. Often we had to explain things to her about South Africa and the world we'd left behind—a phrase, a food—and Dania didn't take easily to needing an explanation for anything. But most of all she was unsettled by Bess's lack of ambition, the waste of her sharp-eyed intelligence on magazines and jokes.

"Now there is ringing again her phone," she said. "Again she must have forgot to take it with her."

"Let it ring. It'll just go through to voice mail."

Dania stood up. "It's like having with us a child!"

I gazed down at the lights along the shore. Whatever Dania thought, I was pleased with the idea of Bess and Dionysos, the mad pull of a man on one's common sense. How long had it been since I'd suffered that mad pull myself? Ages, I thought, and although it was a relief, in a way, to have it gone, still there was pleasure in remembering its power.

Dania burst onto the veranda, holding Bess's mobile at arm's length. "Gledness!" she said. "I do not understand one word she is saying. Is it English?"

⚇

BY THE TIME BESS RETURNED, Dania and I had forgotten completely about Dionysos.

"Gladness is in Athens!" I announced. "What the hell is going on, Bess?"

She flopped down on the window seat. "I know, I know," she said, "but you'd never have agreed if I told you."

"Bess! For God's sake!" I was almost shouting. "Not even *you* can be that disingenuous."

"Shhh!"

"I will not shhh!" Truly, Dania was right. It was like arguing with a child. More than this, her blithe disregard for the ethics of a situation was perfectly in keeping with what I now knew about her mother and grandmother. "Disingenuous!" I repeated. "Insincere! Dishonest! Deceitful!"

She shook out her hair, a sure sign that she was delighted with herself. "I know, I know, I'm a lousy cunt."

Dania lifted a hand like a traffic policeman. "That is a word I do not like," she said. "Please do not use that word, Bess."

"Rex used it as a term of endearment."

"He's also the man who lost for you all your money."

"I know, I know," she said again, trying without success to look miserable.

"And where," I asked, "do you propose to stash Gladness?"

But Bess had it all worked out already, of course. There was the small downstairs room behind mine, where our suitcases were kept. Or, if this didn't suit me, the house just down the hill, the one we were going to rent in June, when the children came. As it turned out, it belonged to Dionysos's aunt, who was willing, he said, to rent out the small downstairs apartment. She could have it cleaned out by Wednesday.

Did the aunt know Gladness was a Zulu?

Yes, yes, of course.

And in June? When the children come?

Well, Gladdy would be there to help, of course. Never mind Wilfred's son, never mind anything, now that Bess was getting her own way.

"I am going to bed," said Dania. "You two must work it out."

Bess waited to hear her door close. "Sorry, Ruth," she whispered.

"No, you're not."

She laughed, entirely happy with herself. "What did she say about Dinny?"

"What have you got to say?"

She arched herself back, staring up at the ceiling. "Did you know he's a poet?"

"I can just imagine."

"No, really. He wrote a book. They sell it in that tobacco shop down there, where they sell the foreign newspapers. He gave me a copy."

"In Greek?"

"Of course in Greek."

"So, what's the use?"

"He'll translate them for me, he says. He translated one already. It made absolutely no sense."

"There's a wife somewhere, I presume?"

"She's off on another island, visiting a sister or cousin or something. Greeks always seem to be darting around from island to island."

"You'd better watch out, my dear. Are there children?"

"A son. In Athens."

"So he says."

❧

DANIA HAD RETAINED A FEW of her patients long-distance. "They count on me," she said, "and, look it, I can make in a few hours on the phone the rent." With one exception, they phoned once a week at a given hour, talked for fifty minutes, and that was that till the next time. The exception was Wendy, and she was a grand nuisance for all of us. She phoned whenever she felt like it, day or night, and every time she did, Dania would snatch up her phone and stare into it as if it were a snake about to strike.

"Daniushka," I said, "why don't you just get rid of her? Tell her to take a running jump?"

"I don't want Bess to know about this," she said, glancing around.

"Why? What's the matter?"

She shook her head. "I was stupid. I took from her some presents."

"*Presents?*" The thought of Dania being won over by Gucci or Chanel was entirely delightful.

"So now I'm caught," she said in a whisper. "Like I have a knife on my throat."

I stared at her. "What presents?"

"It is not professional."

Clearly, but still it seemed impossible. Dania made money easily, spent it modestly, gave it freely to her children and to Amos, the hapless lover she'd married as soon as her divorce went through. "Was Amos behind this?" I asked.

She shrugged. "He wanted badly things, all the time things. Crazy things. Even for her to help us build for the house another floor. And then, at his funeral, she was standing in the front like a wife! Like me!"

"So, just give them back! And the money for that floor!"

"I tried. When I sold the house, I even sent to her a check. But she wouldn't cesh it. And now, if I don't answer her call, she says she has proof—"

"That's blackmail, Daniushka."

"Yes, yes. And she's very clever, too. She hecked my e-mail. Also she took one day a photo of Yael in the boots she gave me— fancy boots from England for riding a horse, can you imagine me? Ruthi, I suffer for this great guilt."

LYING IN THE PLUNGE POOL some weeks later, I mused about Dania and the abiding mystery of her devotion to Amos. He'd hardly been a man at all when she'd first taken up with him. He'd been boyish and sarcastic, and she'd caught him out again and again with other women. So, what was it about him that had had her forgiving him each time? And then boasting about him regardless? What was it about any of us when it came to men? Why, for instance, had I married Clive? Married him without loving him? What had I known then of love anyway? Love, I'd assumed, would bend to my decisions. And, when I found it didn't, there was Hugh to show me the way.

Just as I was winding back to Dania and the situation with Wendy—just as I was thinking that even if we understood the architecture of attraction, still we would never be able to broach the mystery at the heart of it—up onto the veranda stormed a stout, red-faced, middle-aged woman, with Gladness huffing close behind her.

Gladness had been with us for a week, folded neatly into the little downstairs room. It had its own little bathroom, which we'd had Eleftheria scrub clean, and opened onto a narrow side veranda, from which a naked flight of steps led up to the street.

"The lady she knock my door," said Gladness, panting. "She want Bessie."

The woman came to stand at the rim of the pool, chest heaving. She had a thatch of thick, bleached hair, scarlet talons, and small, bearlike eyes squinting into the sun.

Wendy? I thought, climbing out of the pool.

"Missus Beess?" she shrieked at me.

Not Wendy. "Mrs. Dionysos?" I said, hoping Bess wouldn't wake earlier than usual.

She gave a hard laugh. "Missus Beess!" she spat out.

"No," I said, sitting down to dry my feet. "Gladdy, would you show this woman out, please?"

But the woman just wheeled on Gladdy. "Get away, bleck devil!" she screamed.

"Time to go!" said Gladdy, quite unruffled. "You go now, madam!"

And just as I thought the woman would take a swing at Gladdy regardless, Dania appeared in the doorway. "Wot is going on out here?" she said. She cocked her head at the stranger. "Who is this?"

The woman stormed up to Dania now. "Missus Beess?" she said.

Dania gave me her knowing look. "No," she said calmly, "I am Dr. Weiss. You need help?"

The woman swung her murderous glance from Dania to me and back again. And then suddenly, with all of us standing there in silence, she turned and stamped off into the house, Gladdy right behind her. We heard the front door slam, and then out onto the veranda came Gladdy, looking triumphant.

☙

à gg, Greece

Dionysos arrived at the front door one day out of the blue, saying the house agent had sent him to help us with the Internet. She was his cousin, he said, and for any trouble we had we should ask for his help. So, when Gladdy arrived, we asked him please to put up a railing on the outside steps as twice she had almost pitched off the edge.

Safety, in ancient places, is never to be taken for granted, particularly not by women of our age, used to the predictable arrangements of modern cities. Not only do most of the stairs here have no railings, but the steps themselves can vary from an inch to a foot or more high. Cobblestones can be lethal, and thresholds death traps. I have learned to lift my feet like a soldier when I walk through the village, conscious of the dangers about which I've been warned, but never, until now, took to heart.

Dionysos has offered to take us around the island, show us good places to swim, and where to buy the best island ceramics. But when I ask what this will cost, he just smiles and holds up his hands, saying, *Endaxi, endaxi.* Bess finds out that he is a retired ship's engineer, and owns a restaurant on the other side of the island, now closing for the winter; that taxes are iniquitous, and that he'll accept a monthly fee to drive her wherever she wants to go. She also finds out that "ne" means "yes," "yasas" means "hello," and "endaxi" has nothing to do with taxis. It simply means "everything's all right."

Which is what it is on these lovely October days.

෯

THE COLUMN DONE, I CLIMBED up to the main floor for lunch. My middle-of-the-night wakefulness had been returning lately, and not even the boring memoir I'd picked up at the English bookshop about life in the paradise of New Zealand could send me back to sleep. Then there was Gladdy, clattering upstairs every morning just before six to make early morning tea for Bess, leaving her door to blow shut behind her. Up in the kitchen, the clattering of cups and spoons woke Dania, too, who would bellow like a bull. When we complained about all this to Bess, she just said that she'd speak to Gladdy but, really, when you came to think of it, early morning tea was normal for Gladdy, normal for her as well, and couldn't we just get some earplugs?

"Gott!" said Dania. "Arrives this slave with tea before even the sun is up, and this is normal? It's medness."

"Oh, come off it, Dania!" Bess snapped. "You know perfectly well the difference between a servant and a slave!" She seldom lost her temper, but when she did, her fury ran deep. "Do you play these sorts of games with your 'patients'?" she demanded. "Or do you just boast to them the way you boast to us? Your perfect life! Your perfect books! Your perfect everything! Except one of them keeps phoning you, and that's not exactly perfect, is it?" She huffed back on the window seat and pretended to go to sleep.

Dania raised her eyebrows at me. "The nerves of her!" she said. "Ruthi, I'm going to town. Where are the car keys?"

"I'll come, too," I said. "I'll drive."

As far as we knew, Dionysos's wife was still on the island. Enraged wives, Dania said authoritatively, seldom just disappear. Perhaps this one hadn't returned because Dionysos had installed a gate and a lock at the top of the outdoor steps. He'd done this for Gladdy's sake, it seemed, as, clearly, he didn't take his wife herself too seriously. "Maybe I give her a good—" He made spanking motions in the air, roaring into laughter.

"Gott!" said Dania.

What Dionysos did seem to take seriously, for some reason, were the phone calls from Wendy. When Dania swapped the SIM card on her phone, it took the woman only a day and a half to have the new number. Somehow, she also had my number, and Bess's, too. Anticipating one of her sarcastic messages, or even the click of a hang-up, began to make us all jumpy. It was as if she had binoculars trained on us from somewhere across the harbor, a microphone as well. "You all having a good time?" she would say in her girlish whine. "You think I'm even interested?" Or just "Four six five eight (*click*)"—the last four numbers of Dania's new bank account number.

"You know, Ruthi," Dania said as we drove away, "children and grandchildren they don't sound so bad all of a sudden."

I had known that sooner or later it would come to this, and that, when it did, it would be Dania who'd say it. "Then we'd have children *and* Wendy," I said. "It's not either/or, you know."

"And Gleddy," she added. "And wife of Dionysos."

"Those, too."

"Tell me truthfully now, Ruthi," she said. "Do I boast? You think I boast?"

I concentrated on the road. Driving down the hill required all my attention in order to miss the cars parked wherever the drivers felt like leaving them. There wasn't a car on the island that wasn't dented or scraped or worse, including ours. "I should have cleaned the windscreen," I said. "I can hardly see at this time of the afternoon."

But she was looking at me. "I'm asking seriously, Ruthi. I know you will tell to me the truth."

I held up one hand to shield my eyes. "Okay," I said. "You do boast, Daniushka, you can't seem to help it. I've tried to tell you. But not straight. Until now."

She was silent. From time to time, we'd had sessions like this, but usually the questions came the other way, especially when she was suffering an attack of despair. She felt like a failure, she'd say. Just look it—this one had won this, that one had won that, and what had she won? Nothing! Nothing! So then I'd have to remind her about the sixteen books and ninety-two articles, no mention of translations. You're a wonder, I'd say. Just look what you did! The books! The practice! The children!

And then she'd laugh. "Oy, Ruthi," she'd say, "what would I do without you?"

But this time it was different. She'd gone straight to the dark

heart of our friendship, a place we'd approached only once before, when, in a moment of ill-considered candor, she'd told me
that, as far as she was concerned, I had only one flaw: I talked too
much about things I should keep to myself. And even though I'd
recognized at the time that she'd told me the truth, I could never,
through all the subsequent years of our friendship, forget that
she'd scolded me for something that, until then, I'd thought of,
if I'd thought of it at all, as a reckless response to intimacy.

"Sometimes I just like to remind myself," she said now in a
small voice, so unlike herself that I glanced at her to see if she
was crying.

"It isn't important, Daniushka. Really, it's a small thing."

But it wasn't. And she didn't answer.

After some moments, I glanced again. She was staring ahead,
her mouth twisted to the side.

"Maybe," she said at last, "for Gled we can buy in town an
apron like the Greek women wear? Pull over the head? She looks
in that outfit she wears with the cap truly like a slave. What do
you think, Ruthi?"

❧

Ruth, dear, all is well so far. What about if you try to wind in a few of
the challenges you're faced with over there? Nothing too heavy, of
course, just a hint or two so our readers can relate? Sxx

❧

à gg, Greece, SHOWER #1
If we'd thought that, by leaving our lives behind us, we were leaving, in
the mix, the sort of conflicts that arise in families, we were learning to
think again. The bathroom, for instance. Bess likes to shower in the
mornings, and every time she does, she leaves a flood behind her.

Never mind the lessons that both Dania and I have given her in Greek Shower, she can't seem to cope.

As for the cleanup, she doesn't much care about that either. It is one of the things that makes her both delightful and exasperating, particularly if, like me, you are wed to order. And even for me the shower took a week to get under control.

The best way to approach antique Greek Shower, I've found, is carefully. First, just to be safe, you should undress completely, leaving your clothes and all but two towels outside the bathroom. Then, you should close the bathroom door firmly and place one of the towels along the bottom of it, at least for the first few showers. If there is a shower curtain at all, chances are it's cracked, too short, and/or will pull the rod down when you try to draw it across.

Next comes turning on the water. For this, one must take firm hold of the showerhead, unhook it from its noose, and point the nozzle into the back corner of the shower stall. If you don't do this—if you leave it on its cradle while you wait for the water to warm up—the whole thing is likely to leap up, uncoil itself like a snake, and spray everything in the bathroom, including the towels.

Once the water is hot, *turn it off,* position yourself with your back to the corner, and then gently turn it back on, holding the nozzle toward the wall until you have the temperature right. Only then is it safe to spray yourself, remembering never to let go of the showerhead.

à gg, Greece, SHOWER #2
Some people like to place the stool, which usually comes with the bathroom, in the shower stall itself so that they can sit through most of the soaping and showering-down stage. If you do this, bear in mind that, depending on its age, the stool itself might collapse. So, do test it

out before sitting on it. And be warned: even if all goes well through the soaping stage—even if you're vigilant, taking care of curtain, water, stool, and soap—the chances are that, somehow, the bathroom will land up awash anyway, and you'll have to use all your towels to mop up the water.

To none of this is Bess equal. She prefers baths, says she. Well, so do I. Both of us grew up with baths—long, luxurious baths, and sometimes, after a heavy storm, dark and muddy ones. And always there was someone to clean up after us. But, as far as I can see, the nearest bathtub seems to be in a Turkish bathhouse several islands and a sea in the direction of Turkey. And so, I have pointed out to her, we're simply stuck with Greek Shower, at least in this house.

We have four bathrooms, one for each bedroom. This is because the house started out, about forty years ago, as a small hotel. And for forty years not much has been done to improve the plumbing.

None of this seems to bother Dania. She's an old hand at Middle Eastern Shower, says she, and is also quite easy with the hole-in-the-floor toilets one still finds in some of the old public buildings, and which neither Bess nor I will consider, never mind Dania's assurances that they are easier, cleaner, and better for the constitution. If Dania would simply use the things and not emerge to deliver another boast, we might even find it all quite funny.

❧

BY THE TIME GLADDY WAS in the aprons Dania and I had bought her, the unpleasantness had subsided among us. No one brought up the boasting again, Dania stopped using the word "slave," and even Wendy seemed miraculously to have disappeared. Her phone calls and e-mails stopped. She was gone.

But Dania was wary. "I have had before psychotics in my practice," she said. "I refer them to a psychiatrist. But this one wouldn't go. She is fixated on me."

"Oh, don't worry!" said Bess. "Dinny probably fixed things, although he pretends he knows nothing about it." She was always promoting the benefits of Dionysos's presence in our lives. And now that he'd put up the railing and gate to keep his wife out, she said, would I consider swapping my suite downstairs for hers up here? That way she wouldn't have to come through the house and disturb us when she came in at night.

I leapt gladly at the suggestion. The upstairs rooms were lighter, with better views. I'd only volunteered to take the downstairs one as I'd thought it would be quieter. But, with Gladdy clattering around there, and Bess calling down to her every five minutes, or shrieking for help when the bathroom flooded again—well, both Dania and I were rattled to the bone.

Gladdy and Bess had an arrangement between them that was like nothing I'd ever experienced, not even in childhood. To anyone looking in on them, it would have seemed quite clear that Gladdy was the one giving the orders. "You already got a stain on that dress, Bessie," she would say, clicking her tongue. "You need an apron like mine." Or, "Go away now, Bessie. You making more work for me here."

And so up Bess would come, rolling her eyes happily at us.

The fact was, though, that we'd all come quite quickly to rely on Gladdy, even Dania. Every morning Gladdy caught the bus down to the port to buy produce and cheese from the farmers lined up along the marina. She also bought fish from the fish man, and meat from one particular market that had the freshest supply—much cheaper than London, she said. And she'd made a friend of the woman who weighed and priced the produce, the same one who ran the juice machine. Before she'd arrived, I'd been buying bottles of freshly squeezed orange juice every time I went to the market. But once Gladdy found out how much I paid, she put a stop to that and took over the squeezing herself.

Wherever she went, Bess said, Gladdy made friends. What's more, she was shrewd about it. Just look how she'd taken to wearing that cross around her neck. People here didn't know one black from another, Gladdy had pointed out, and she didn't want them mixing her up with those rubbish North Africans selling drugs on the pavements in Athens. So, every Sunday she dressed up and made her way with the village widows to the local church. The service itself she considered a sorry tuneless affair and the priests terrifying with their beards and ponytails. She passed the time reading her Bible on her lap, she said, and singing hymns to herself—"All People That on Earth Do Dwell," "O Jesus, I Have Promised," and so forth.

Until her grandson phoned one morning, I'd completely forgotten that Gladdy even had a family of her own. But now there she was, the phone clapped to her ear and her voice rising into an eruption of Zulu outrage.

I looked at Bess. We were sitting together on the window seat, listening like children to the tirade neither of us could understand. "They only phone when they want something," Bess whispered. "Drives Gladdy mad."

"Ai, suka!" said Gladdy at last, snapping the phone shut. "Rubbish boy! Rubbish country!" She thrust the phone into the pocket of her apron and slammed off into the kitchen.

As it turned out, he'd phoned to say that the pills weren't working anymore for his HIV, and would Gladdy please send money for a private doctor?

"He probably sold them," said Bess, "and you know what's going to happen? Just watch! She's already paid the bond for him twice—petty theft, breaking and entering—never mind that Patience has a job and drives a Mercedes, the selfish cunt!"

Suddenly it occurred to me how much of our freedom depended on the health of our children and grandchildren. Unhappiness? We could cope with unhappiness. We could also cope with resentment, and even hatred. It was illness that was the terror—accidents, assaults, all those unforeseen things that could come along and cut down a life in a moment.

"And if he dies," Bess went on, "there'll be the funeral to pay for, just you wait and see!"

I closed my eyes against the tumble of horrors taking possession of my thinking. Rogue drivers, suicide bombers, vicious rapists, madmen with guns, head-on collisions. I got up and went to my room. *Tell Lily to be careful!* I e-mailed Hester. *Remind her to look both ways before crossing the street regardless of a green light. When teenagers move in a feral pack, they lose all common sense. Even Lily.*

But my concern only delighted Hester. *Oh, Mum!* she wrote back. *You're the one who should be looking both ways, for God's sake! What's going on there? Want me to come and rescue you?*

☺

Hester #2

I knew, of course, that the week at Club Med was going to be awful—I just hadn't imagined how awful. Already on the bus from the airport, Hester was slapping on makeup I didn't even know she possessed. By the time we arrived, three hours later, she'd transformed herself into a plump tart—her skirt rolled short at the waist, her hair loose and wild, and her eyelids blackened into wings. She made a point of elbowing forward to clamber off the bus ahead of me, and would have disappeared into the crowd for the entire week had we not been forced to share the same room.

As it was, she slept through breakfast and was gone by the time I returned. For all I knew, she was sleeping with a new boy every hour, and ahead would lie venereal disease, abortions, God knows what.

I would sit on the beach, trying to ignore the incessant thump of the music and wondering at the strangeness of this new turn in my life. Sitting there, with the smell of tanning oil and the salt air, the sound of the surf, and the warm sand under my feet, I was crippled by a hopeless longing for Africa and the life I'd left behind all those years before.

Returning to America with Hester after the cold, gray damp of London—leaving behind all the small arrangements of our lives there—had seemed, somehow, a move closer to the ease and familiarity of that life. It would be a way, I'd thought, of blunting the longing I still suffered for those few months I'd had in Hugh's bungalow before she was born—of reviving, perhaps, the defiant good fortune of finding myself at home there, even briefly, even after he was murdered.

But if he'd lived to see her born? Would that not have brought down the romance regardless? How many romances could I think of that had survived their children intact?

❧

AND THEN, ONE DAY, JUST as Dania had expected, Wendy showed up again. "Ruthi!" Dania whispered urgently. "Come in here! Close the door! Look! Read that!" She pointed to the screen of her laptop.

"But it's in Hebrew."

"Yael writes in Hebrew because there came for her an e-mail from that vapor in the grass. About Amos and those women."

"Listen," I said, dropping my voice, "never mind the women. Amos is dead. You're just going to have to call Wendy's bluff."

"How? *How?*"

"Tell the truth! Yael's your daughter, for God's sake and, really, what can happen to you? You accepted presents from a patient, you accepted money—it was extremely stupid, but surely not worth all this? Why don't you just tell all the people you're so worried might find out? Wouldn't that be better than having the woman stalking you? Because, really, that's what this is, you know—stalking. Hacking into your bank account and e-mail? Daniushka! For God's sake! It's illegal!"

She shrugged. "I knew it was impossible such a woman should disappear," she said. "Now she goes after Yael again. She wanted already her son to marry her, can you imagine? He is also psychotic."

"Dania!" I said, raising my voice. Really, this transgression of hers, this lapse of judgment, or cowardice, or weakness—whatever name one gave it was nothing to this blank refusal to face up to the situation she'd put everyone in—it was widening into a crack, a moral chasm. "Blame Amos! He might be dead, but he is equally to blame!"

"And Yael? She likes too all those fancy things."

Bess popped her head around the door. "What's going on in here, you two?" she said. She had an uncanny way of hearing voices dropped to a whisper.

"Wendy the stalker is in Paris now," I said. "She tracked Yael down there."

Bess came in and settled onto the bed. "What's Yael doing in Paris?"

"She can in one day be here," said Dania. "It's easy for her. She can go anywhere she likes. She's got from her parents a fortune."

"*Who?*" said Bess. "*Yael?*"

"Not Yael. That woman who torments me."

"Oh, her!" Bess lay back on the pillows. "What's Yael doing in Paris?"

"She likes to brush on her French."

Bess snorted.

"Maybe you should go and see Yael in Paris," I said quickly. But really I was thinking, What was to stop Yael if she decided to come and see Dania here? Never mind our rules? And then the others found out and decided to hop over themselves? What then? I'd already heard the question in Hester's voice when she'd announced that Lily might go to Spain for a summer abroad. In the pause that followed I'd seen myself on the ferry to Athens, in the taxi to the airport, and then traipsing around the Acropolis with Lily in the heat, trying to drum up some interest in the girl's passion for horses.

Somehow, things had been easier while the children were still resentful. Now that they were beginning to thaw—now that Wendy had thrown herself back into the mix—there was no knowing who would turn up next.

"What's the woman got on you?" Bess said, staring hard at Dania.

Dania shrugged. "There are things I can't talk about."

"So, why worry then?"

I looked at Dania. I wasn't going to help her with this. "I'm going for a walk," I said, wanting some time away from both of them.

"Oh, I'll come, too!" Bess said. "I just have to put on some shoes."

There were days like this in normal life, I told myself as I waited for Bess outside—days in which nothing came right, not even a solitary walk. And yet, free of the life I'd left behind, and of Hester and her headlong quest for a way to bring me to my maternal knees, why couldn't I feel free? Why, in the middle of the night, did I still wake as if in terror, with my heart thudding in my chest?

"Won't be a sec!" Bess shouted up the stairs. Even readying herself for a walk, it was as if she were undertaking a hike up Kilimanjaro.

While I waited, I gave another try at Emptying the Mind, something in which Bess and I had both been instructed by Agnes, her daughter, and at which we'd both failed hopelessly. There we'd sat, cross-legged on the carpet, with Agnes issuing instructions in a dulcet voice. They were nothing alike, Bess and Agnes. Agnes was pale and long-boned, with an antic, mirthless smile. "Eyes closed," she'd said, and obediently Bess and I had closed our eyes. "Now empty the mind."

But it had been impossible to empty my mind, and it still was. The minute I emptied it of Dania and Wendy, I found myself considering dinner tonight, and that Dania and Bess would, as usual, be happy with gyros, whereas I wanted grilled calamari at Halaris—although what I really longed for was a gorgeously roasted chicken, much more expensive in Europe than in America. So maybe I'd ask Gladdy to pick one up at the market to-morrow, which would be too late for the bananas we needed for breakfast. I'd tell Bess we had to make a stop at the little food stand on the square, however irritating it was to be the only one of us who ever seemed to think ahead.

I looked at my watch. And what if I don't think ahead? I asked myself. What, in God's name, would happen if I failed to remember bananas? Or that the car needs gas? *Be in the moment*, Agnes had told us in the way of the mind-emptying Californians she embraced. But what moment? The minute you were *in* one moment, it had passed and the next was upon you. Which was where I was now, waiting from one moment to the next for Bess to put her bloody shoes on and come out for the walk I'd wanted to take alone.

And then, suddenly, standing there, I thought of Stefan Gripp, and how I'd made such a big deal, after eleven Gripp novels, of killing him off in the grand finale (that spectacular choking incident, modeled closely on Amos's demise), timing the end of the series so nicely with my escape to Greece—that I could hardly admit to myself that I was lost without him. But of course I was. Every day for twenty-five years I'd been waking to the thought of what would come next—book to book, year to year. And now this.

I buttoned my jacket against the late afternoon wind. What, if anything, I wondered, could settle me into enjoying this so-called freedom I'd so exultantly wrested for myself? Allow me to wake up to it with delight? Walk about with it? Enjoy the length and the breadth of it, not just with a glass of ouzo in the evening, but also in the afternoons, right here, right now? Not waiting impatiently as I was, a priggish aging malcontent thudding with irritation because her dear old boastful friend had exposed herself in the face of petty blackmail as a coward and a fool—just waiting, with the sort of ease and contentment that used to come after hours of labor, and seemed so hard to find without it, even in Greece?

"Here I am," said Bess, puffing up. "By the way, we need bananas. I ate the last one this morning."

❧

à gg, Greece

One of the things that is hardest to take about Greece is the toilet paper situation: used toilet paper must not be flushed, it must be deposited in a bin next to the toilet, often quite full already. Even though the bins themselves usually have lids and pedals—even though one is warned that the sewage pipes are ancient and narrow and that violating the toilet paper rule can land the toilet, restaurant, hotel, or house in a sea of sewage—the custom invites furtive flushing. Somehow, preserving used toilet paper seems like a sin against toilet training itself. And decency. And, really, ew, that bin!

But there it is in every toilet: "Pleas! No Paper In Toilet"

The only one of us who complies absolutely is Dania. She considers Bess and me rather suspect in our fastidiousness, although, three months into our time here, she's less prone to saying such things outright. So we tell each other toilet stories. When she climbed Kilimanjaro, she says, one of the bearers actually carried a toilet on his back for the tourists. I tell them about my old lover—the one I still miss from time to time—how he only cleaned his toilet when he knew I was coming over, and even then did such a lousy job of it that I lined the seat with paper and took care to keep my clothing off the floor. Mushrooms sprouted around his bathtub. And, when he went to bed, he tied up his garbage bag and put it in the freezer to keep it from the mice.

Ew! they said. Ugh!

Considering him now, depositing used toilet paper in a bin seems rather mild. After all, you'll never see it again. And as long as everything else is clean, so what? Just think of the sort of women who are too fastidious to sit on a toilet seat at all, and poise themselves over it. How many times has one had to wipe down a wet toilet seat in the women's restrooms of America? Keep one's pants from touching the floor? By all rights, such women should be confined to hole-in-the-floor toilets, and then made to shake hands with the sort of women one encounters in French lavatories, emerging from the stall and making straight for the door without benefit of soap and water.

By contrast, Greek toilets are spotless. And anyway, as Greeks are quick to tell you, the whole arrangement is the fault of the British, who laid down the sewage pipes in the first place. And, let's face it, the Brits aren't so hot on cleanliness themselves.

۞

STANDING ON THE UPSTAIRS VERANDA in the early morning, looking out over the sea, I felt open not only to the sea and the sky, but also, somehow, to the past and the future. The light on the island was like the biblical light of the world, the town itself the biblical city built on the hill. Early each morning I went out there, when Dania and Bess were unlikely to join me, just to feel open in this way. And then, standing there one morning, it occurred to me that this—*this*—was what Agnes had meant, this emptiness. Except that it wasn't empty—it was full of possibility. And it was the closest I had come in the forty years since leaving South Africa to feeling at home.

۞

LONG AFTER WE'D ALL FORGOTTEN Dionysos's wife, in she stormed again.

"*Missus Beess?*" She stood in the middle of the living room, fastening her gaze now on Bess herself.

If Bess hadn't looked up from her mobile and raised her hand like a child in school, the woman might well have thought she'd missed again. But, as it was, she stormed over to the window seat like Artemis on the rampage, and stood there shrieking incomprehensibly as she tore up some pages she'd been clutching, ripping them into furious confetti and hurling them over Bess.

Bess was just sitting up to brush them off when the woman leaned forward and spat at her in a great torrent, missing her face but catching the sleeve of her caftan. Then she gave out a loud derisive laugh, rolled into another volley of invective, wheeled around, and stormed back out through the front door, slamming it so hard that it bounced open again.

For a few moments we all stayed where we were, staring at the door in case she came back. But when she didn't, Bess sat up, pulled her dress over her head, and threw it to the floor. "Could we *please* keep that door *locked* in future?" she said.

"Listen," I said, regaining my breath. "I told you she'd be back. We're only lucky she didn't bring a weapon."

Bess lay back, abundant in her bra and matching thong. "What can he possibly see in that bleached pig?" she said to the ceiling.

"Melina Mercouri maybe?" said Dania, who had never quite got the hang of rhetorical questions.

Bess's mobile binged. "What now, for God's sake?" she said, staring into it. "What!?" she shouted. "WHAT?"

Dania looked at me. *What now?*

"They send this in a *text*?" Bess cried.

"What?" I said. "Send what?"

"*Wilfred* and that *Tarquin* of his!" She looked up as if she'd just remembered we were there.

"Duckwin?" said Dania. "It's a name, Duckwin?"

"They're going to *adopt* the child!"

"I thought they'd already adopted one?" I said. More and more it was becoming clear that our children didn't have to be with us in order to disrupt our lives.

"They *did*! They *have*! But that tart of an au pair is refusing to have an abortion—"

"Gott!"

"Yes, *Gott!*" Bess snorted.

"Well, better for Gladdy the new one will be white, no?" said Dania breezily. "Maybe now she can go back there to help?"

"Oh, for God's sake, Dania," Bess said. "This is *not* funny!" She stood up, hands on fabulously naked hips. "It's about as unfunny as that 'patient' of yours. Perhaps you should tell us now what she's got on you? It might help when *she*, too, comes storming in here."

Dania glanced at me. *You told her?*

But Bess caught the look. "What's going on between the two of you anyway?" she demanded, turning her fury on me now. "I feel as if I'm in kindergarten again."

"Nothing to do with Ruthi," Dania said quickly. "I did a stupid thing, that's all. But I can't talk about it."

"*Why not?*" said Bess. She went back to the window seat at last and sat there, one bare foot twitching like the tail of a cat.

Gladdy came in from the veranda, the gate key swinging on its chain around her neck. "Hey, Bessie, why you nekkid like that?"

Bess snorted. "There's spit on my dress. Please put it in the wash."

"Spit?" Gladdy picked up the dress and inspected it. "Who spit on you?"

"Just make the tea," Bess said haughtily. "I need some cake."

Before Gladdy had arrived, we'd bought baklava, almond cookies, and rich, honey-soaked cake from the bakery in town. But now, every week, there were jam squares, or butter biscuits, or sometimes, like now, a Victoria sponge with vanilla icing. When I marveled at their familiarity, Bess just laughed. "They should be familiar," she said. "They're your grandmother's recipes. Our grandmother," she added. "She gave them to the cook at the hotel. Isn't it funny how the grandmothers had to meet like lovers? Isn't it romantic?"

I smiled as I always did but, really, it wasn't funny to me, and certainly not romantic. When I thought now of the way my mother had questioned my father, the flaming rows they'd had behind the bedroom door, there was a deep stab of pity for her. Had I known the reason then, I'd have blamed him myself, taken more notice of Bess when her grandmother brought her for tea. But, as it was, if I'd considered Bess at all, it had been as an oddity—a wild child brought up in a hotel by her grandmother, no parents in sight.

And yet who was I to be so fastidious? I, who'd had my own love child all those many years before? One rule for everyone else, none for me? Probably so. The fact that I'd detested Clive—I knew now how deeply and broadly I'd detested him—had been irrelevant. I'd been married to him; I'd taken Hugh as a lover and had had his child. And if Hugh had had a wife in the mix, I wouldn't have blamed her for storming in and spitting on me herself.

◎

Ruth, dear, the toilet edit works well, but could we now move on from showers and toilets to something more of the order, say, of Greek cuisine? Sorry to be confusing, but when I said normal life I didn't mean take out the big guns :) That recipe for the marinade brought in a huge response, by the way. More of same? Another thought: I'm hearing that some of those islands are known for the longevity of their inhabitants. Could you look into this? It might do for a few columns—say, women versus men? Diet? Exercise? We'd pay expenses, of course, within reason. Sxx

◎

à gg, Greece

Cats in Greece, like cats everywhere, know just how to arrange themselves to best advantage: under restaurant tables, along the tops of walls, in the shade of a church. But stay here for more than a summer and you learn that they lead desperate lives. There is not enough food for them, or shelter. And so, during the winter, most of them sicken and die, or are drowned by the locals. There are cat rescue organizations, of course, and sterilization campaigns, but how can they keep up? One female cat and her kittens can produce five thousand cats in four years, they say. Is it any wonder then that one seldom finds an old cat in Greece?

Still, I saw one yesterday—an old gray shorthair with the tip of one ear missing. He was snoozing on an upholstered bench at a popular outdoor restaurant and, when I tried to unseat him, opened one eye in warning and then went back to sleep. I tried again, but this time he let out a low warning growl. So I took the chair next to him and glanced up into the enormous ficus overhead to see whether there might be any more up there, just waiting to leap.

There weren't. And I was sipping my Greek coffee in the afternoon heat, enjoying the sight of the foot traffic going past, when suddenly the cat leapt up and flew over my lap like an enraged panther. He was after a dog that was approaching quite casually with the stream of tourists. Seeing the cat, the dog skidded to a stop, spun around, and fled, his tail between his legs, with the cat in wild pursuit. After a while, the cat returned, jumped up onto the bench, curled up again, and fell asleep.

◈

IT WAS AFTER GLADDY TOOK off for South Africa to see to her grandson that Bess, restless without her or Dionysos, began to say she might go back for a visit herself. We'd been in Greece for five months now, she pointed out, and the weather had turned, which meant that most of the restaurants were closed for the season and, really, what was the point of Greece when the sun wasn't shining? she said. It was depressing, that was what—wet and cold and gray, almost as bad as London. Anyway, she'd only be gone for six weeks, and would still, of course, be paying her share of everything—just keep a tally, and wouldn't Dania and I enjoy some time to ourselves? For old time's sake?

There was no point in arguing with her, I could see that. I'd learned over the months that when Bess brought up the possibility of doing something, it was a way of preparing us for the fact that she'd long since made up her mind to do it.

"Of course you go!" said Dania. "Of course, of course!" Clearly, the prospect of six weeks without Bess delighted her. "Gladdy is not so terrified in that country anymore?"

"She is, she is. So, that's another reason. She's terrified in Patience's flat. So, when I'm there, she'll come and stay with me. I've found a B&B for us up the coast, in some sort of compound, with gates and walls and guards and God knows what. Much too dangerous to stay along the beachfront anymore, I hear."

"How far up the coast?" I said, suddenly thinking of Hugh's bungalow, long since knocked down to make way for just such a gated community.

"Beyond Umhlanga, maybe up where you were, near the sugar estates."

I smiled. It had been over forty years since I'd lived in Hugh's bungalow, and still it was the place and time from which, for all these years, I'd felt most exiled. I glanced at Dania, wondering how to say what I suddenly wanted to say—that I wanted to go myself; that we could all go, and so what if we closed up the house here for six weeks? What did we have to lose except a stalker and a crazed Greek wife?

And then, as if on cue, Bess looked up and said, "Why don't you two come along? I've looked into the airfares—really, they're not bad if you go via Cairo or Istanbul. You could think of it as a holiday from a holiday!"

Dania frowned. "One minute that country is too dangerous for Gladdy, and the next we must all go because there are gates and walls? It's too crazy."

෧

à gg, Greece

The grannies are on the go again, at least two of us are, this time to South Africa. Dania decided not to join us. Her daughter and grandchildren will come to Greece for their Christmas holidays, giving her a chance to see them without violating the rules we set up at the start. She'll also have time to write what she now categorically calls her last book (number seventeen, but really number nine, not counting translations).

Meanwhile, we are receiving a lot of comments via *So Long* from women who feel the need to straighten us out on the subject of grandchildren and, not incidentally, to assure us as to how much they treasure their own. "Our lives are busier since grandchildren," writes one, "but my husband and I wallow in the joy of it all. Between our time with them, we swap stories about them with our friends who have grandchildren."

How to respond to such a declaration? And do I dare to correct the grammar? Or do I simply enter into the competition and assure this happy granny that I, too, am really, really, underneath it all, wallowish about my grandchild, banking up stories to lob at the other grandparents I know?

What I've found is that there's no winning in this arena. Apart from which, there is something so bleak to me in the lives I imagine behind such declarations that I begin to feel quite bleak myself. I am still feeling bleak when Hester, my daughter, Skypes in on Sunday evening at the usual hour and I have to drum up questions for my sixteen-year-old granddaughter, whose eyes keep dropping to the mobile on her lap. When Hester scolds her for this, it is I who come to her defense, because, really, the exercise is exhausting for all of us, this strange new world of grandmotherdom.

☙

THE B&B BESS FOUND TURNED out to be a "guest house," although the distinction between the two was unclear to me. Whatever the case, this guest house did not allow children under the age of fourteen, and so there was no screaming around the pool, no whining at meals, none of that—only a few decorous teenagers (a surprise in itself) with their parents. They were shy in the old-fashioned way, blushing, awkward, and so a pleasure to observe.

The day after we arrived, I rented a car, and found that de-lightful as well. Forging off on my own without Bess or Dania to accompany me, I sang as I drove, and when I returned, there would be Bess, waiting for me. She and I had fallen quite natu-rally into parallel rhythms. She spent her days under an um-brella at the pool, or called for a taxi to take her to one of the many malls that had sprung up around the city.

Until I'd met her, I'd thought of myself as a natural shopper. But I saw now that, for me, shopping was just a pastime—desultory, sometimes profligate, occasionally triumphant, and quite often fraught with remorse. For her, on the other hand, it was more like a calling. Even there, where the things that would normally have interested her were few and overpriced, she took life from the hunt, returning to the guest house with a new set of sheets, hand embroidered with local flowers, or last season's Italian clutch, three times the price she could have had it for in America. And so what? she said. It happened to be in just the shade of mustard she'd been after, and doubtless would be off the shelves everywhere but on eBay, which she didn't trust for one minute.

As I saw it, once she'd seen something she might like, she couldn't stop wanting it until she had it. And if, after a few days, she looked at it and thought, What did I get this for, it's just another thing?—still, if she hadn't grabbed it when she'd seen it, it would have haunted her until she had.

In fact, going to South Africa turned out to be lovely for everyone but Gladdy. She spent her days at the hospital, where her grandson was dying. It was too late, she reported, for the doctors to help, even the expensive ones. And Bess had been right—he'd sold the pills Gladdy had bought for him over the years. Every day she zipped her money into some sort of contraption

that she tied around her body, and caught two packed mini-
buses to the hospital. There she'd feed him spoonfuls of soup
from a can, or Coca-Cola. She washed him and changed the
sheets because conditions in the ward were terrible, she said,
terrible. Still, it was hard to tell what his death would do to her,
what his life had meant to her either. If you mentioned his name,
she just clicked her tongue and waved away any answer she might
be expected to give.

Everything was difficult for her in South Africa, even break-
fasts and dinners at the guest house. She sat straight-backed at
the table, refusing to look at the menu, which she pushed over to
Bess. "You do it for me, Bessie," she whispered, and then pressed
her lips into a dignified line to shut the subject down.

The truth was, she was lost there now, just as she'd known
she would be. The two gorgeously overdressed black couples staying in the penthouse suites disconcerted her. Everyone disconcerted her, even the waiter who brought the glass of water she'd
ordered on a silver tray. "What he needs a tray for?" she whispered
furiously when he'd gone. "Why he can't just carry it without
showing off?"

On the weekends, Patience came to fetch her. She was large,
very large, and as sullen as I'd imagined she'd be. If Gladdy
wasn't ready and waiting, she'd lower herself into one of the
wicker chairs in the hall, and there she'd stay, her bag on her
lap, responding to offers of tea or coffee with a sullen shake of
the head. Perhaps she disapproved of the bargain her mother
had made with domestic service. Or of the bargain that had
been made for her. Had she been pleasanter about it, I'd have
found a way to tell her that I didn't blame her in the least for
this. And I didn't. But, as it was, I simply nodded to her and
walked on.

"She's always been like that," Bess said. "She blames me, of course. And my grandmother. Poor Ma—I called her Ma, you know—I do wish I hadn't named Agnes after her. But how was I to know she'd turn out to be a life coach, for God's sake? Ma would turn in her grave."

◉

Hester #3 (HUGH)

The first time Hugh Stillington had brought me out to the bungalow, I hadn't been ready for his world. I'd sat on the veranda thinking of things to say as he'd dismissed the servants in perfect Zulu and then poured me a sherry from an old cut-glass decanter.

"Do you imagine you'll be comfortable in America?" he'd asked over his shoulder. With five generations of sugar behind him and a reputation for righteous reform, he was miles from the vulgarity of my own world and its contempt for anything local.

Everyone else had accepted without question that, with Oxford behind me, I was going to America to get some more degrees, a clever girl like me. I had almost come to believe it myself. The whole plan seemed to fit well with Clive's green card, and with the way he kept apart from the sort of doctors ready to take a wife. Just as I stood apart from the sort of women who majored in psych and socio and announced their engagements just before graduation.

◉

FOR TWO DAYS, I'D BEEN driving up and down the coast, looking for the road to Hugh's bungalow. But it had gone—road, bungalow, even the old hotel. When I stopped for tea at one of the newer hotels and asked a grizzled old Indian waiter if he remembered it, he just shook his head. "People," he said, "are always coming looking, and finding nothing, because nothing is staying the same, madam, am I right?"

I nodded, although, as far as I was concerned, he was quite wrong. All these years I'd told myself that the life I'd left behind was gone, place and people. But, despite the upscale lobbies and infinity pools, the high-rises and thruways and malls, here it still was—scones for tea and, out there, two fishermen on the rocks, the sun on the surf, frangipani and hadedas. Sitting there in the familiar afternoon light, I was as happy as I'd been for a long time.

And Hester? I wondered, pouring myself another cup. How much love had she wrested from the two hopeless men she'd driven into and then out of marriage? It was hard to tell. As far as I could see, her real love affair was with the father she'd never known, the life she might have had, the life he might have given her. Now that I was here, she'd begun talking winsomely of meeting me here herself—bringing Lily, perhaps, and what did I think?

What I thought was that by the time she'd sorted out the details, I'd be back in Greece. I went to stand on the balcony, watching the last of the light on the sea. By all means, darling, I'd said, see what you can do.

❧

à gg, Greece

One small cause of relief in being away from America is that no one either here or in Greece seems moved to declare love at the close of every telephone conversation. "Don't forget the dry cleaning! Love you!" "No, you may not go to Sarah's house today, you have homework to do! Love you!"

I have tried to work out when and how this plague began, but every time I ask American friends, they are either embarrassed—wondering, no doubt, whether they themselves have committed this folly with me— or they shrug. When I asked a student at a crime fiction conference why, at the end of every line of dialogue, she had her narrator adding the phrase like a tic, she looked at me as if I'd just spat on the flag. "But what if the other person's actually *murdered*?" she said. "And no one's *told* them?"

So, I gave up.

Bess's daughter has taken up the tic with a vengeance. There isn't a phone call between them that doesn't have Bess swearing as she snaps her mobile shut. "Loves me!" she cries. "Do you think she's being sarcastic? I mean, that might give me some hope. There I am, in the middle of telling her this life-coaching business is a toss, and she says, 'Got to run! Love you!'"

I shrug, only glad that Hester hasn't yet taken it up. Lily did try it out on me once, and when I didn't join in the volley, was left a bit bewildered at the other end. She's sixteen, probably trying out what she's heard others say, and who better for the purpose than a grandmother?

But not this grandmother. I would have felt cheapened saying it, ridiculous, ashamed. Love, I could have explained, was a private, costly, complicated thing, full of uncertainties, full of hope. Between a grandmother and her grandchild there should be another word for it—something calmer, taking into account the charm of generation, the vagaries of chance.

I could have told her that in another era I might have been living in her mother's house or she in mine. Whether we liked each other or not, there we'd be, making our peace with biology. After a while, her mother would have a commode brought in, special nappies, bottles of baby food. And when, at last, it was time for me to leave, and my hand— more like a claw by then—reached out for her to say goodbye, she'd shrink from it in terror, retreating to the doorway, lest I try to take her with me.

◈

RETURNING ONE MORNING FROM TOWN, Bess plonked a box down in front of me. It was large and old and tied up with string. "You won't believe it!" she said. "She locked it up in the bank!"

"What?" I said. "Who locked up what?" I was almost getting used to the way she landed in the middle of a subject, expecting others to follow.

"Ma!" She untied the string and lifted the lid. "Just look!" she said. "Money! And all sorts of other stuff. Open it!"

I looked and, yes, there, neatly stacked, was bundle upon bundle of banknotes, each tied up in its own piece of brown string.

"She left instructions that it should be given to me when she died, and the bank chap said they sent a letter, probably to the old address. And just as well I didn't get it, I suppose, or the ex and late and unlamented would have put it into a trust fund for the children. Or Rex would have gone through it. Either way."

She lifted out a bundle of notes. "Let's count."

"Bess," I said, "you should put it in the bank. It's dangerous to have this much money lying around here!"

"The chap at the bank said it was a shame it had been sitting there so long as it had lost half its value. Is there a room safe?"

I tied the string up again. "Even if there were, it wouldn't be safe. And I seem to remember there are laws about taking cash out of the country. You need advice."

"I know, I know. But isn't it wonderful? And you didn't even see the photos."

"What photos?"

"Underneath. There's a pile of them."

I untied the string, opened the box again, and took out the bundles of money, lining them up carefully on the bed. And there at the bottom was, indeed, a stack of photos, and also a stack of letters—all, it seemed, written in the same bold, heavy hand.

"That's not her writing," she said. "They must be love letters. Let's have a look!"

"First, we should put the money in a plastic bag," I said. "Something inconspicuous that could look like lunch. Then I'll drive you to a bank."

❧

THE LETTERS WERE MARVELOUS, FULL of elephants and natives. If I had found them before I gave up on the Stefan Gripp series, I could have used them there. So what if I brought him back to life somehow? I thought. Now that I was so at sea? The column counted for nothing against the great maw that faced me day after day. Less than nothing, in fact. Even Bess had her shopping, and Dania had her phone calls. In fact, Dania, of all of us, seemed the most content with this time of life.

Writing to her, I didn't mention the money Bess had found. Although it was in the bank now, there was still some question as to how she'd get it out of the country without paying a ridiculous forfeit. There was also the funeral of Gladdy's grandson to pay for; it couldn't be more than a week or so off. And after that, Bess said breezily, we could just come back again every year—she, Gladdy, and I—until the money was all used up.

❧

WHEN THE TIME CAME, BESS hired a van and driver to take Gladdy, Patience, herself, and the grandson's body up to Gladdy's village for the funeral. It was a ghastly experience, she said—appalling hotel, heat, noise, cockroaches—and as for the funeral itself, all that wailing and screaming, and Patience, who hadn't even bothered to visit him in the hospital, loudest of all—well, only Gladdy had really wept, so full of sorrow and true misery, and *why*, Bess kept asking, *why*, when all Gladdy had ever had from the boy, start to finish, was trouble?

"Everything she's lost was there," I suggested. "Everything she could have belonged to."

"We're all lost," Bess said. "What could be more lost than me living with Agnes? In America? What could be more lonely? No money, no lovers, no glamour, nothing. All that's left is Gladdy." She sat up. "And I don't want to read those letters," she said. "I knew Ma the way I knew her, and I don't want to know now what I didn't know then." She tossed her hair. "She had all sorts of lovers, you know, your grandfather was only the first of them. That's probably where I got it from."

I laughed. I knew she thought I could do with a lover or two myself. "It would cheer you up," she kept saying. "Look how Dinny cheers me up. It's like having a small heifer following me around. Do you know he calls me 'Gina'? For Gina Lollobrigida?"

I smiled, wondering who I might have been to Finn. Every now and then an e-mail still came in from him, probably after a few glasses of wine or because he was at loose ends. And sometimes there would, indeed, be a pang for what was gone out of my life—what, in fact, I didn't even want back—except for the lovely sense of being seen again by a man, longed for, loved. When I watched men watching women now, all I could think was how biological it all was—this need, this game—and a shiver of the chill of death would run through me.

"I have another idea," Bess said. "Why don't you write one of your columns about Dinny and me?"

I laughed. "Why don't you do one yourself?"

"Me? Don't be mad!"

"But, really, why not? It's only about a page and a half. Just write whatever you like."

She laughed happily. "But where would I begin?"

⌀

à gg, Greece

Bess here. I've been thinking a lot lately about being fat, and that, when it comes to men, fat has never had anything to do with it. It's your face they're after, and your happiness they want for themselves. They also want praise, of course, but we all know how to play that game. Just think of a dog. Because, really, they're just dogs, dying for a bit of a pat, and when you're my age it's the old dogs you'll get, sitting there, wanting something to wag their tails at.

Talking's another thing that has nothing to do with it. If Dinny had been able to talk to me properly—I mean more than, You like? You okay, dulleeng?—it would have spoiled things. Anyway, I didn't want to know his story, I've heard quite enough of men's stories already. I knew he had a wife, of course, but that's only a good thing because when men have wives then you don't have to wake up to their groping and bad breath. You just have the candles and the wine and an hour or so later they're looking at their watches and dressing to go home.

It all goes fine, of course, until the wife finds out, which they always do because the husbands want them to know, even if they don't think they do. They're so proud of themselves, you see, and for years the wives have hardly even noticed them as men. So why not give them something to be sorry about?

I look at the beautiful young girls in the mall and around the pool, with their skin, their hair, their laughing, and I feel like all the men in the world looking at them, and also all the girls in the world being looked at, including the girl I was when men first started looking at me. So, you see, it doesn't really matter that I'm a fat old cow now. It all just makes me want to sing.

☙

Ruth, dear, marvelous idea to have each of you do some columns. This one from Bess is a really good start. I'll send the edit. Sxx

☙

"*WHAT?*" BESS CRIED. "Just tell me why 'wanting something to wag their tails at' is worse than 'wanting someone at whom to wag his tail'? Mine's better! *Miles* better! I mean, what's she after with 'at whom'? I *hate* 'at whom.' Would *you* say 'at whom'? I wouldn't, not with a gun to my head." She huffed around in her chair. "'*At whom*'! I ask you!"

I laughed. She was even more possessive of her prose than I was of mine. And, anyway, she was right: hers was better. And I loved her for it.

"And *why* did she put in 'and I'm not unhappy with that' after 'I'm a fat old'—WHAT?? She changed 'cow' to '*woman*'! How can she do this? Did you tell her she could do this? Well, just tell her I want 'cow' back! And who said anything about being unhappy? And no! NO! I will *not* explain why it makes me want to sing! Is the woman so stupid that she can't work that out for herself?" She flung up her hands. "Listen, Ruth: Is this what you have to go through every time? Because if it is, no wonder you hate it. It would drive me around the bend."

☙

à gg, Greece

Greek coffee—or Turkish coffee as the Turks would have it—is one of the delights of life in Greece. It isn't hard to make, but you will need what they call a briki—a small pot with a handle, preferably copper. And be sure to buy Greek coffee, which is very finely ground for this purpose.

Using a small demitasse as a measure, fill the briki with cold water for the number of demitasse you need. Then add one or two large teaspoons of coffee grounds for each two-ounce cup of coffee, depending on how strong you like it. If you like it sweet, add one or two teaspoons of sugar per cup. Heat the briki over medium heat, stirring to mix coffee and sugar. As the coffee heats, foam will rise. When it almost reaches the top, remove the briki from the heat, using a mitt or a cloth (the handles are not insulated) until it subsides. Let this happen three times before turning off the heat. Then allow the coffee grounds to settle.

To serve, pour a little foam into each cup and follow with coffee. Serve with a glass of cold water. The coffee should be sipped very slowly, like a liqueur.

The miraculous thing about this coffee is that, although it is every bit
as potent as regular coffee in America—more potent, I am told—it
does not keep me awake at night. When I ask Dionysos about this, he
just gives me his broad, charming smile. "It is because is Greek,"
he says. "Everything Greek is good!"

☙

WE'D BEEN BACK ON THE island for a week, and it was as if
we'd just arrived again—Would you mind? and, If it's not too
much trouble? Even Gladdy couldn't seem to relax back into the
way she'd been before. Certainly she wore the aprons and made
the early morning tea, but her cheerful bossiness was gone, and
more than once I heard her click her tongue when Bess called
out for her. Still, when I suggested that perhaps she should have
had time at home to mourn, Bess just shook her head. "It's not
home for her anymore," Bess said. "No sooner was the funeral
over than she started nagging me to leave."

"Maybe she just doesn't want anymore to be here a slave?"
Dania suggested.

Bess shrugged. She knew by now that Dania wasn't being
provocative. In fact, Dania reported that she'd been turned into
a slave herself when Yael came to stay. "Every morning, six a.m.,
the children came so Yael could get for herself another hour of
sleep, can you imagine? And, oy, the shouting! The fighting!
They're adorable, of course, but around the corner comes June
and they'll be beck! Thanks be to Gott Noam is phobic about
flying or for sure he'd be coming, too, and Esther in her sheitel,
and those children, can you imagine?"

"Would you consider doing a column on that?" I said. "You'd
make less than you do for an hour on the phone. But it might
be fun."

"You're kidding me! You don't put in print things that will come back to bite you."

Bess frowned over her glasses.

"I know, I know," said Dania. "I'm bitten already. So maybe I do one about the husband who is choking to death on a marshmallow?" She gave one of her hearty laughs.

"A *marshmallow*?" Bess said. "I thought it was steak?"

"No!" cried Dania, laughing truly now, almost crying with laughter. "I said steak because a marshmallow—" She collapsed into uncontrollable shrieks and snorts. "It's hard to die a funny death," she said at last, wiping her eyes.

Bess was laughing now, too. It was the first time, in all our months together, that I'd seen the two of them showing any signs of real friendship. "How the hell do you choke on a marshmallow?" she said.

"He was playing with them a stupid game, like a child, putting so many into his mouth, counting up." Dania threw up her hands. "Amos was a child. I was married to a child."

"So, write about *that*," said Bess.

But suddenly the joke was over. "Maybe one day an article," said Dania soberly. "The eternal boy playing the games of children, and Mommy doesn't stop it."

"And watches him die?" suggested Bess.

Dania looked up sharply.

"But you did, right?" said Bess. "I mean, marshmallows are soft. You could have tried to pull them out?"

❧

BY JANUARY GREECE DIDN'T SEEM like Greece anymore. People huddled along, bracing against the wind and rain. Even Bess, who claimed to thrive in cold weather, complained about how bleak it was. "One misses the lights," she said. "And the furs. And they didn't do much about Christmas either, did they?"

"They pay more attention to Easter," I said, looking up from the hideous scarf I was crocheting for Eleftheria. She'd chosen the yarn herself—green, purple, and silver. Since she'd been replaced by Gladdy, I'd gone out of my way to maintain the connection in case we needed her when the children descended.

"Well, let's hope things cheer up soon," Bess went on, "or I'm going to go to Athens for a break." She grumped down under the rug she now used on the window seat.

"Better check the ferries," I said. "If the wind's too high, they cancel. FYI, you can wear your furs there."

"'FYI'! Next you'll be saying *love you!*, and then I really will go to Athens," she said.

I laughed. "If you go, would you get me some wool? I mean real wool. All they have here is this awful multicolored acrylic stuff."

She tossed her magazine to the floor. "How many variations on 'How to please your man' can they think up year after year? And, anyway, who cares about pleasing them? I'm sick to death of pleasing them! Do they ever wonder about how to please *us*?"

༄

à gg, Greece

Stuck in the unheatable marble sitting room, with the rain outside and hours to go till dinner, we've all been rather grumpy. Greece in the cold and rain isn't the Greece we came here for. The restaurants are closed, the beaches deserted, and old men occupy the cafés, smoking like fiends.

This morning, Bess tossed her magazine to the floor, and said, "Why do they keep hammering on in these magazines about how to please men? Who *cares* about pleasing men?"

Well, none of us, as it turned out. We are all rather sick of pleasing anyone, and dead bored by the subject of sex. So, quite soon we'd meandered away from the idea of pleasing men and onto what men could do to please *us*.

"That's obvious," said Bess, picking up her magazine again. "Romance. It's sweet, and funny, and gives you something to look forward to."

Okay, we said, but only for a while. And even Bess had to agree with this.

"Money," said Dania, "is what most women want. To be secure."

We discussed this for a while—what we'd be giving up for such security. And, again, we decided it wouldn't work, at least not for us. We were lucky, we said. Here we were in Greece, each of us independent of those sorts of obligations.

And then it was my turn, and, out of nowhere, came the answer. "Listen," I said, sitting forward. "All a man has to do is utter four words, and we'd be his completely."

"Words?" said Bess. "Who wants words?"

"What words?" said Dania, looking keen.

"'Leave it to me,'" I said. "Just let a man say 'leave it to me,' and we'd follow him anywhere."

☙

"REX IS THE ONE I MISS," Bess said one day, "even if he is a crook. I don't even mind about the au pair anymore, although I was ready to kill him when I found out."

"You don't mind the money?" said Dania.

Bess looked out into the rain. Perhaps, after a lifetime of being forgiven for her own desertions, she found it easier to forgive one in a faithless lover, I thought. Or perhaps the one didn't follow the other. Probably it didn't, and it was simply that she didn't suffer as much as other women. I liked this idea. It fitted, somehow, with the way nowhere seemed to hold her too tightly, not even South Africa, where she'd come and gone with neither nostalgia nor regret. Perhaps she was simply deficient in deep feeling, I thought. But if I taxed her with this, she'd only say, Shallow? Of course I'm shallow! I've always been shallow.

"He wasn't even much of a lover," she said now with a sigh. "This position, that position—like Pilates."

"To them performance is important," Dania said. "We must clap."

"Or shout and scream," I said. "That was Clive."

"French men love shouting and screaming," said Bess. "Very noisy in hotels."

"Trouble is, he wasn't French," I said.

"What about those skinny ponytails that make them feel not so bald?" Dania said.

"Nothing wrong with bald," said Bess. "In fact, I like bald— all that skull under the skin."

I looked out at the rain washing across the veranda. It was almost as depressing as the conversation.

And then my phone rang. I looked at my watch—the middle of the night in California. "*Hester?*" I shouted. "*Hello?* What's the matter?"

"So, what've you got to tell me?"

Finn? It was impossible.

"Finn!" I said. "For God's sake! Where are you?"

"Finn?" mouthed Bess, not inaudibly. "The garbage-in-the-freezer man?"

"Where do you think I am, you old cow? Down here at the dock, getting wet. Come and pick me up immediately."

I hung on, breathing lightly.

"Well? You coming, or do I have to find a taxi?"

"Wait where you are." I snapped the phone shut.

"Hester must have told him," I said. "She's moving from passive to active aggression."

"But where is he going to stay?" said Dania. She'd never seen the point of Finn, although she stopped just short of saying so directly.

"We can put him down the hill, where Glad was going to be," said Bess. She'd come alive suddenly with the news. "We've got plenty of extra sheets and towels and so forth."

"No," I said, putting on some lip gloss. "We're not putting him up anywhere. He can go to the hostel, it's the only place that's open. And probably the only place he can afford."

"With the students?" Bess said. "Oh, this gets better and better! Let's all go down to pick him up!"

"Uh-uh," I said. "I'll handle this alone."

❧

HE WAS STANDING IN THE wind as I drove up—spare, pale, a little more bow-legged, but still rakish in the battered old safari jacket I'd given him years ago. He peered into the car. "Good," he said, throwing his bag into the back and hopping in. "Pleased to see me?"

I'd forgotten the ripe smell of him—old sweat, old beer, the fake almond scent of his shampoo. I coughed.

"Got something to eat?" he said as we drove out through the gates. "I haven't had anything since breakfast."

I'd forgotten, too, how sure he was that I would care whether or what he'd eaten. "Why didn't you have something on the ferry?" I said, knowing perfectly well he must have saved himself even the cost of a sandwich. "We can stop at a restaurant if you like."

"Somewhere cheap?"

"Everything's cheap here. But, listen, you're either going to have to stay in a hotel down here, which is cheap, or at the student hostel up where we are, which is cheaper."

He looked at me. "You don't have a couch?"

"Hester told you where I was, I presume?"

"I told her not to tell you."

"She didn't." How typical this was of Hester, I thought—she who'd never much liked Finn, but liked my new unencumbered life even less.

I parked the car. "There's a nice café along the lane there," I said, remembering how, suddenly, he would be shot through with romantic largesse and would take me without a thought to a fabulously expensive restaurant. "You can leave your bag in the car. I'll lock it, but no one steals anything on this island. Finn," I said, "you're not going to just pick up here where you left off three years ago, you know."

☙

BY THE TIME I HAD dropped him off at the hostel and come back to the house, Dania and Bess were wild with curiosity.

"Where is he?" Bess demanded. "You're not going to hide him away, are you?"

I fell into a chair and kicked off my shoes. "Hide him? Are you joking? He's not going to let himself be hidden. Listen, what am I going to do with him here? I'm serious."

Dania gave me her judicial frown. "Ruthi, you must be

clear with him. You must set the limits. He is not here your guest."

Always, when she started this sort of thing, I longed to remind her of Amos and of all the other leeches she'd carried through the years one way or another. In fact, Finn wasn't a leech, and I'd never carried him anywhere. "The thing is," I said, "he'd give me his bed if the situation were reversed, and he'd sleep on the couch himself."

"I can't wait to meet this paragon!" Bess cried. "Mine takes my money and charters a yacht, yours gives you his bed!"

"Right!" said Dania. "Finn gives to you something that costs him nothing, Ruthi. And it keeps you where he wants you—in his bed. You can't see that?"

I waved the question away. If I could have waved them both away with it, I would have.

"And with the breast cancer," Dania went on, "where was he then?"

"What's this?" said Bess. "What breast cancer?"

I shrugged. "They caught it early. And he found all sorts of reasons to absent himself. So I absented him permanently. Sort of."

"But that's just what men do," Bess cried. "Of course they're not there when you need them. That's where the children come in."

She was right. It was Hester who'd warmed to the situation, setting up a bed for herself next to mine, driving me to and from radiation.

The doorbell rang, the knocker thumped, and Gladdy shuffled out from the kitchen. But before she could get to the door, he'd tried the handle and come in.

"Who forgot to lock this time?" said Bess, sitting up. "Hello? Finn? My, you're not at all what I expected!"

He stood where he was, smiling around the room. His hair was completely gray now, but thick and well cut. "Better or worse?" he said.

"Better! Far better! Wow!"

Don't bother to flirt with him! I thought. He's appalled by fat women—by fat anyone, in fact.

But then there he was, loping over to the window seat and settling himself opposite her, not even a nod at me or at Dania, whom he'd never liked anyway.

"Seen the rooms in this hostel place?" he said. "Closest I've come is the Trappist monastery where Merton stayed."

"Merton who?" Bess never minded showing off her ignorance, especially in the presence of a man. She tucked her legs up under her dress. "What's a monk's chamber like? What are the monks like? Are they all gay?"

Gladdy was standing in the kitchen doorway, observing closely. How many times had she gone through this with Bess? I wondered. Watched her come alive in the presence of a man? And then fly off with him, leaving her to take over?

I stood up, heat rising to my cheeks. "Finn," I said, "you haven't said hello to Dania."

"I'll say hello when I'm ready to say hello," he said, still looking at Bess. "You're English?" he asked her.

Dania pushed herself up and came over to the window. "I haven't seen you since Ruthi had the surgery," she said. "You're going to stay long in Greece?"

"Haven't decided." He hardly turned to look at her.

"Oh, stay!" Bess cried. "We're bored out of our minds here!"

"Speak for yourself," said Dania, still standing over them. "You're only bored since Dionysos went away."

"Since *who*?" Finn cocked his head.

"The taxi driver," Bess said. "He's a darling, but the wife isn't."

There's a misstep, I thought. Finn had an old-fashioned reverence for marriage. In fact, he'd always thought that marrying me would wipe his record clean.

"What's she look like?" he asked.

"Bleached, fat, almost as fat as me." Bess looked around. "Is it too early for a drink?" she asked.

⟜

à gg, Greece

Twenty years ago, if a man who had once been my lover took up with a friend of mine, I should have had her eyes out first, and then his. But something wonderful has happened in old age: I look on in bemusement. The fact that Bess, who detests walking, has taken to walks with Finn down to the bar he's found near the cathedral; that she, who brought her own down pillow because how can she be expected to sleep on anything else, now finds nothing to object to in his narrow pallet at the hostel up the road, and will even climb the four steep flights of marble steps, all 185 plus pounds of her, to get there—well, it has me waiting every evening for what comes next.

How they both fit onto that pallet is another matter. I can't quite bring myself to ask her this, probably because I have lied, telling her that her size never occurs to me. Maybe there are two pallets that they push together. Whatever the case, I have no doubt that she's paying for him to stay there. So maybe this is what has made her the exception to his strong aversion to fat women. Even when his own daughter, who'd just delivered a baby, took some time to slim down, he asked me to talk to her about it. "Couldn't you suggest a diet?" he said.

Well, no, of course I wouldn't suggest any such thing, any more than I'd now tell Bess to watch out, the man was using her and she was going to land hard—harder for all the weight she carried—when he let her down.

Dania says we should suggest they take off together while the going's good, taking Gladdy with them. Which would leave Dania and me in the house alone and, really, the more I think about it, the better it sounds.

๑

WITH BESS GONE MUCH OF the time now, Gladdy was like a lover left behind. She still shopped and cooked, but in a desultory fashion, and largely so that there'd be a cake for Bess when she came back for tea, or soup in the freezer, or the moussaka she'd learned to make from the cook down at the hotel. It was even for Bess's sake that she'd overcome her suspicion of eggplant. There she was now, salting and oiling it for roasting because Bess had particularly asked for an eggplant and feta salad.

"Gladdy," I said, "what are you going to do if Bess goes back to America with Finn?"

She clicked her tongue. "I phone Wilfie last night. He says he will come."

"When?" I said. There were months to go till June.

She shrugged. "Maybe I phone Aggie, too."

"Glad," I said, "you know they're not supposed to be here until June?"

She turned back to the eggplant. "Bessie she must grow up now. She's an old woman, like me."

This was as close as I'd ever heard Gladdy come to criticizing Bess in earnest.

"Finn he's your man," she went on, "not hers. Why she takes someone else's man?"

"He hasn't been my man, as you put it, for some years now."

She looked up. "Someone they need to chase him away."

Clearly, she'd given it all some thought, and was taking Finn far more seriously than she had Dionysos.

"If she stopped paying for him," I suggested, "he'd probably have to go."

She clicked her tongue again, but said nothing. I'd had the feeling from the beginning that she thought Bess a cut above Dania and me, and that the money Bess had been born to had something to do with it.

"It's funny," I said, "because he doesn't usually like fat women."

She looked up sharply. "Something wrong with him?" she said. "Like Wilfie?"

It was a divine idea. And if Wilfred did arrive, so much the better. Finn found gay men almost as distasteful as fat women.

In the meanwhile, there was no knowing when he and Bess would come back to the house, except in the mornings, when she came back on her own to shower and change. If he came with her, he'd sit in a chair with one of her magazines, flipping through it, snorting derisively, tossing it aside. Then he'd lope into the kitchen to try, yet again, to win Gladdy over. But she pretended not to notice him. Or, if she couldn't, she answered his questions with grunts and shrugs. If he asked her for some water, she'd give him a glass and point to the tap, no question of his using our store of bottled water.

Strangest of all was that it was Dionysos who was driving both Bess and Finn around the island now. He'd arrive at the front door just as he had in the beginning, reeking of cologne. And then off they'd go in his old Mercedes, the three of them, Finn in front, all talking and laughing as if Dionysos had never been anything more than a taxi driver to Bess from the start.

And yet, watching them, I couldn't help wondering why I had so steadfastly retired Finn from my life. If Bess was right— if all men let you down when you needed them—might not Hugh have done the same one day? Hugh, who, by dying so soon, had become my touchstone for all things best about men? So, why not this man? This funny, penniless man who had me suddenly feeling robbed of his laughter and his love? Even though I'd been turning him away and away over all these years, and hadn't missed him until now—now that he was here? It was ridiculous. But here I was, ridiculous at sixty-nine, looking in on their happiness and feeling like an abandoned girl.

And yet, I told myself—and yet he had come here for me, not for Bess. And he hadn't even given me a chance to reject him. Which, almost certainly, I would have. Or probably would have. It was hard to say, watching them go off together for yet another dinner somewhere on the island, what I would have done.

"Does he know," said Dania, "that the last one took most of her money?"

I shrugged. "The funny thing is he's never been the sort to go for women with money. Or, at least, I don't think so."

"Who knows what such a man wants? In this case, she goes for him, and he's gone. Ha!" She sat back, pleased with the construction.

But she was getting on my nerves now, almost as much as Bess. "What do you think attracted Amos to you?" I asked.

"Amos?" She shrugged. "A rotten piece of *sheet*. I'm *gled* he died."

I stared at her. Dania hardly drank, and never took so much as a sleeping pill. I'd never heard her like this.

"When I saw him choking on those marshmallows, I didn't jump up. I sat where I was. I smiled at him." She gave out a hard guffaw. "He was waving with his arms and pointing with his fingers to his throat, digging in there, too, but I just sat where I was, waiting for him to die."

"*What?*"

"I did, I did! He was a *sheet*," she said again. "He even went to bed with that crazy bombashell who stalks me."

"With Wendy? I don't believe it!"

"You don't believe with those breasts and that money and those glued nails she could get him? Such a bombashell for that pig? I say they must have been good pigs together!" Again, the guffaw.

And then suddenly, I understood. "Daniushka, did she know about the choking? Daniushka," I whispered, "did you tell her?"

At last she returned to herself. She rubbed her eyes. "She took like a thief whatever she liked. And she liked Amos. But then I had enough. So I told to her myself the news he died. And, boy, did she scream and cry! And when again she asked, I told her again how, just to make her scream and cry some more. And that time she was recording it."

"God!"

"Yes, Gott! So that is why I can't call her a bluff, as you say it."

❧

I SAT OUT ON THE veranda, observing the cat on the roof down the hill. Every evening it sat there, still as a shadow, watching the pigeons swoop and turn, and then swarm back to their dove-cote. It was a melancholy sight. Were Finn with me, he'd blame the melancholy on the moon. He set great store by the phases of the moon. But, moon or no moon, if I told him what I'd just heard from Dania, he'd sit up sharply. Didn't I tell you about that woman? he'd say. Didn't I tell you to stay away from her?

❧

Ruth, dear, we're wondering if you can redo the piece on Finn and Bess, play down the weight issue a bit. We love the idea of your "bemusement," but can you go with that rather than her heaviness? It sounds a bit snarky. Sxx

❧

à gg, Greece
Have you ever noticed how delicately fat people eat? At least in public? A bite of this, a bite of that, and then the discreet chewing, eyes darting to the buffet table to make sure there'll be enough left for seconds?

We were all invited to the annual feast on Easter Sunday. It was a community affair and, because the weather was fine, it was held outdoors in the square. Enormous spits had been blazing since dawn, roasting lamb. And there were trestle tables laden with food. It had been brought in from all over the island—Easter breads, bright red hard-boiled eggs, cheeses, soups, olives, potatoes, pies, salads—a gorgeous display.

Bess and Finn were already there when Dania and I arrived. They'd found seats within easy reach of the buffet, and Bess was already taking her tiny bites, Finn sitting rather awkwardly, I thought, beside her. He's always been scathing about fatness, loud and scathing, and now there he was, with Bess lifting and lifting her fork, and Gladdy, also fat, behind the buffet, helping the Greek women serve.

With Gladdy, though, also a delicate eater, I don't have a sense of greed behind the fatness. Or of lust. Or even of relish. I have the sense of a woman making do with what life has dealt her, and waiting out her time until she can be reunited with her Lord.

Standing there with the other women, with none of whom she can hold more than the most rudimentary of conversations, Gladdy looks more at home than I've yet seen her. She is concentrating on carving into the haunch of meat before her, laying out the pieces on a disposable platter. And when Bess wambles up with her empty plate for thirds (or fourths), Gladdy doesn't look up and smile as she's always done. She just goes on with her carving. So Bess has to choose the juiciest bits for herself.

☜

NO SOONER WAS EASTER OVER than Wilfred appeared, striding in, with Tarquin behind him carrying the child. They were an odd trio—Tarquin, tall and pale and tattooed, an earring in one ear and his head completely shaved except for a fence of gelled gray coxcomb down the center; Wilfred, much older, short, ovoid, and balding, nothing like his mother; and then the child, a beautiful black pearl of a baby, almost as plump as Wilfred.

"Wilfie!" Gladdy cried. "You get too fat!"

He took Gladdy's hands in his. "Fat old tart yourself, leaving us in the lurch like that!"

She laughed merrily. "Hau!" she said. "You too rude!"

Bess waved from her usual place on the window seat. A few days before, she'd moved back without any notice, and still seemed a bit mystified that Dania and I hadn't welcomed her warmly. "Is that the baby?" she said vaguely. "What's his name again?"

Wilfred turned to Tarquin. "Darling," he said, "take Mohammed down to the hotel while I deal with my mother."

The hotel had not been due to open for some weeks, but somehow Wilfred had talked the manager into letting them in, at least for the time they'd be there.

"I told him he couldn't come until June," Bess said to no one in particular, "but did he listen? Has he ever listened? Ha!"

"You listen to me, Ma," said Wilfred, settling himself into a chair, "we will come when we please and stay for as long as we please."

He was a hateful little man with a hateful, whiny little English voice and close, pale, hateful little eyes. According to Bess, he'd been hateful from birth—hateful when she took off with her lovers, and even more hateful when she returned. A bully and a cheat, she said, just like his father.

She glanced around, hoping, it seemed, for some help from Dania or me. "He could've gone anywhere for a holiday," she said lightly. "So, why here?"

He laced his fingers together. "Do you want to hear it again?" he said. "Now? In front of your friends?" He was nothing like Bess, nothing like his sister either. Agnes, without the sort of New Age Renaissance garb she favored, was a tall, clear-skinned, large-boned beauty, much like the great-grandmother and namesake I'd seen in the photographs.

Bess tried a laugh, shaking out her hair. But her flush gave her away, cheeks and ears and neck. "What about some tea, everyone?" she said. "Gladdy?"

"Look, Ma," Wilfred said, leaning forward, "at the rate you're going you'll be on the dole before autumn. Do you know how much you're overdrawn? No, of course you don't. You've never even bothered to answer my e-mails."

THE LAST LAUGH   73

"Gladdy?" Bess said again. But Gladdy was clattering tea things in the kitchen now, the kettle beginning to whistle.

"I won't save you this time, you know," he went on, "and neither will Aggie. I've seen to that."

I glanced at Dania. Nothing Bess had told us could have prepared us for this.

"So, this is what I've done: I've arranged a debit card for you. In fact, I've brought it with me—here it is." He slapped it down on the table between them. "A certain amount will go into your account every month, and that's it. If you want to take on another fancy man—although I gather this one is anything but fancy—he'll have to carry you this time. I have also instructed Spottiswood to freeze the overdraft, which is just about at maximum anyway. And, by the way, I've discussed all this with Aggie, and we are entirely in agreement. Neither of us will contribute another cent."

At this he stood up and, as Bess had made no attempt to reach for the card, bent and flicked it a few inches toward her. "We'll be dining at the hotel tonight," he announced.

❧

AFTER THE DOOR SLAMMED SHUT, we all sat in silence, like survivors of a mass attack.

"Hau!" said Gladdy, coming in with the tea tray. "Wilfie he's gone?" She cocked her head. "You fight with him again, Bessie?"

"You brought him here!" Bess shouted, sitting up. "You're the one making all the trouble! You're a traitor!"

Gladdy shook her head. "Hai!" she said. "Don't talk lies, Bessie!"

"I know!" Bess went on. "I know you phoned him! Do you think I'm *stupid*?"

I looked on as she struggled, trying to imagine her without her money behind her. But it was impossible. Even after Rex had made off with the bulk of it, she seemed to wear it about without a thought, spending wherever she felt like it. And now here she was, the debit card staring at her from the table, as if she'd been forsaken by the gods.

⊚

à gg, Greece

We were never the sort of women to divide the bill according to who had ordered what. Right at the beginning, and because Bess wanted to feel free to order and eat and drink as much as she pleased (which was a lot), she insisted that she put in half to our quarter each for all food purchases, including restaurants. She was so insistent about this that we finally gave in. But, when Gladdy arrived, we wouldn't consider allowing her to increase her share, although she did make a good try at doing so. Every month, we deposit the money into an account we'd opened at the bank in town, keeping some cash in the coffeepot for Gladdy to use when she goes to the market.

I have thought a lot about money since we entered this arrangement. What would we do, for instance, if one of us didn't have enough? And how long would the others carry her before resentment set in? For years now, women have been suggesting to each other how marvelous it would be if we could all live together when we were old. The reigning fantasy is built around a compound, a physical compound, each of us living separately, but within reach of the others. Where this would be—with some of us for the sea and others for mountains, some for hot and others for cold—we didn't bother to decide. Nor did we discuss the disparities among us, most important of which was money. None of us, it seemed, tended toward socialism, and so we just chatted on, never coming to any practical conclusions.

And now here we were, living out a version of the fantasy, and still there was no real talk of money. Dania and I had equivalent amounts to see us through, accumulated variously from our books, our retirement, the rent for the houses we'd left behind. If we didn't live to be a hundred, we said, we'd be okay. But Bess was another matter. She'd inherited her money from her grandmother and had never had to think how difficult it had been to come by. When she found that most of it had been lost by a feckless lover, she hadn't seemed to think much about it then either. And neither had we, until it finally ran out.

I SAW FINN AT THE bus stop as I drove past. He looked silly, standing there among the tourists and, like a silly girl myself, I felt a bit sorry for him. But only a bit.

And then, down at the port, there he was again, loping along toward the ferry terminal, his bag slung over his shoulder. I turned back toward the café, but too late. "Hey!" he called out. "Didn't you see me at the bus stop? Aren't you even going to say goodbye?"

It had never been easy to ignore Finn. I was always somehow in danger of laughing, even when things were anything but funny.

"Hey!" he said again, crossing the road, mindless of the traffic. "You've been avoiding me. That's not nice when I came all this way to see you."

I got the car door open and deposited the box of baklava I'd bought.

"Why are you being like this?" he said, loping up behind me. "You know you're the only woman in my life."

People were turning now to watch us from under the café umbrellas. Some were smiling.

"Go home, Finn," I said, low and clear. "No one wants you here."

"No one?" He peered down at me. "Really?"

I'd written about women in stupid situations like this, and now here I was myself, secretly pleased with the game. "I'm expecting Dania," I said.

"That woman is out of control," he said, suddenly sober. "Best to send her back to where she came from."

"Dania?"

"I didn't say her, did I?"

"You didn't say anyone. You said 'that woman.'"

"Well, I meant the other one. And you can take that or not." He wheeled around and made off, back toward the ferry.

I watched him go. He had always been like this, refusing to utter the name of someone he didn't like. Dania had been nameless for years. And now it was Bess? Doubtless, he considered her to blame for the failure of his magnificent gesture in coming to see me—she, and now her homosexual son behind her. Sooner or later, I knew, he'd decide we were all to blame—that we'd been against him from the start. When I'd told Hester that he'd gone off with Bess, she'd rolled into a fit of hysterical laughter. "Did you kick him out?" she'd said. "Did you hurl his slippers after him?" She'd always adored the slipper-hurling scenes, and when finally Finn was kicked out for good, that's when, with the coast clear of rivals, she'd felt free to lay claim to me herself.

As the weather was fine, I walked down the alley to the café, sat at the cat's table, and ordered a salad and a beer. If I stayed in town for lunch, Bess might be gone by the time I went back up. But where would she go, she and Gladdy? Back to London? I couldn't see Wilfred agreeing to have them. And yet, how could she stay on here? And, if she did, how would I cope with her?

There were a scant three months left before the children would start to arrive, and already they were trying to adjust the rules. What if they came for our seventieth birthdays? Hester had asked. Dania and I were weeks apart, and surely Bess could be talked into celebrating two months ahead of time? Anyway, earlier would suit Hester because of Lily's riding camp. And Agnes was keen to come at the same time so that Lily could babysit. Lily herself would be glad to earn some extra pocket money, she said, so how rigid were the rules?

I took a swallow of beer. Yael, Wilfred, and now Hester and Agnes, all of them arriving when they weren't supposed to. At least Noam wasn't coming. And maybe Wilfred and Agnes wouldn't come at all, I thought, now that Bess was on her beam ends. I stared down into the salad. It was still too early for tomatoes, I should have thought of that. I should have thought about Bess, too, before so impulsively including her in our arrangement. As it was, we'd all been so full of hope—stupid, thoughtless hope—so pleased with ourselves for our escape that we hadn't considered anything like this. But who could have thought up Finn? Or Dionysos? Or Gladdy? Or even how empty the house would feel without Bess and Gladdy in it?

☾

Hester #4

*Perhaps if I'd actually seen Hugh's body after the murder—
brains and blood, the nostrils slit to ribbons, one eye out of its socket
(I invent these things; all I know is "stabbed")—perhaps then I'd have*

felt the loss more violently. If I'd even thought he might die, perhaps
I'd have tried to notice things about him more carefully, things to
remember for the future. But, as it was, all that was left of him that first
time I revisited the bungalow was his absence. The place without him in
it. The peacocks gone. Dust on the binoculars. Cobwebs in his boots.

I'd watched Hester walk onto the veranda. At fifteen, she'd had
his wide shoulders and sinewy arms, but not his careful deliberation of
movement, the float of the head. And, suddenly, watching her there, I
felt the loss of myself as I'd been with him, and turned away, pinching
the bridge of my nose between two fingers.

☙

DANIA AND BESS WERE STILL there, just as I'd left them, the card still on the coffee table.

"It was never me Finn wanted, you know," Bess said as I came in. "I knew all along it wasn't me." She looked up, hoping, I knew, for a miracle that would return things to what they'd been before.

"Maybe it's too late to be knowing things all along," said Dania.

But Bess ignored her. "What if I do another 'Granny' piece for you, Ruth? I mean about him, you, and me?"

"I did one already."

"*Really?*" She sat up, suddenly brighter. "May I read it!"

I waved off the question. Somehow, with her so desperate for forgiveness, the charm was gone out of the whole idea of revenge.

"I could write about how antic he is," she said. "Like a grass-hopper."

I laughed, I couldn't help it.

"And how he announces what he's just about to do," she said, a bit encouraged. "Didn't you find it funny?"

Clearly, she expected me to forgive her as quickly as she'd forgiven Rex. Well, I did and I didn't, one minute to the next. But if anyone was going to skewer Finn, it was going to be me, not her.

"Look," said Dania, "soon we should be discussing the money situation."

"I sent an e-mail to that banker in South Africa," Bess said quickly. "I told him not to worry about the exchange or penalties or whatever it was, just to send it. So it'll be okay, see?" Her voice was uncharacteristically high, and her body seemed to have collapsed into a mound.

"Maybe we talk about this when Wilfred is here?" said Dania.

"Are you *joking*?" cried Bess. "I hope you're joking, because if you aren't, you're just being a bitch."

"Gott! Did you hear that?" Dania turned to me. Color had risen to her cheeks and neck.

"Of course she heard it!" Bess shouted. "She's sitting right next to you, for God's sake!"

I didn't want to be pulled in, and I didn't want to talk about money either. "I'm going for a walk," I said, standing up. And before anyone could think of joining me, I added, "Alone."

◉

à gg, Greece

It took Wilfred, Bess's son, to chase off her new lover. He's always been resentful of her lovers, she says—resentful of everything, especially being left so often with Gladdy. As far as Bess is concerned, he was better off with Gladdy, they both were. She herself had never had any interest in children, her own or anyone else's. Why, she asks, do women claim to fall in love with them so automatically? She didn't. She didn't even try.

So now she is not only without a lover, she's also without money. And clearly she blames Wilfred for both, somehow. Were he more appealing, one could feel sorry for him with such a mother but, as it is, it's Bess I feel sorry for. There is something enviable in her particular brand of unapologetic selfishness. What she wants she wants with a passion. Perhaps she'd once wanted the father of her children this way, or even the children themselves, although I rather doubt that.

Dania, on the other hand, envies none of this. And clearly feels herself superior to someone with such a son—gay, married to another man, the father of an adopted black child. What do you expect? she says. It was Gladdy who was in the place of a mother to him.

She doesn't hear herself when she asks this, and I wonder what she sees when she looks in the mirror. When I stand in front of it, I can almost forget the eyes and the skin and the mouth as I try to disguise them with makeup. But what about what's not in the mirror? The sag of the buttocks? The breasts? The sorrowful knees?

And what does Dania see? Once she was gorgeous, a wild-haired Magyar in her gypsy jewelry and sandals. She would slip her lovers into the house at lunchtime, when her husband was at the university and the children at school. Does she remember this now? I wonder. Does she miss anything about that time of her life?

⊚

WILFRED WAS FINISHING HIS BREAKFAST when I came into the dining room. "Want some tea?" he asked. "Gladdy!" he shouted. "Put the kettle on for another pot!"

Seeing him sitting there, commandeering not only the teapot but Gladdy along with it, I took hold of the back of a chair to steady myself. "How long do you plan to stay on the island?" I said.

He lifted his chin at me. "As long as it takes to convince Gladdy to come back with us," he said.

"But Gladdy seems to prefer staying here, with your mother."

"Well, she may find she has no choice. Glad," he said, when she came in to fetch the pot, "I'd like you to look after Mohammed this afternoon while Tarq and I drive around the island—"

"Ruthi," Gladdy said quickly, "I bring your *bakkyva* now? Some juice?"

"Baklava?" Wilfred raised his eyebrows in an exaggerated show. "Why didn't you tell me there was baklava, you old tart?"

"Only one left," she said. "For Miss Ruth." She seemed to reserve "Miss Ruth" for crises, small or large, although Dania was always Miss Dani. Otherwise, I was Miss Ruthi or, if she felt particularly pally, just Ruthi.

"What about this afternoon then?" he said to her. "Can you do it?"

"How did you come to choose the name Mohammed?" I asked quickly, wanting to save her.

He sighed dramatically. "There's going to come a time, you know, when he'll be asking you how you came to be named Ruth."

"That would be quite easy to answer," I said, seating myself at the other end of the table.

"Glad!" he shouted, scowling at his watch. "Go and wake Ma up, please!"

She came fussing in with my baklava and juice. "Wake her up yourself, Wilfie," she said. "Too bad for that, hey?" And off she went again, cackling to herself.

I looked over at the gleaming white houses on the hill opposite, the ancient terraces descending to the port. There were dozens of islands just like this one out there, I told myself. If it came to it, I could just pack a bag and ferry over to one of them for a few days, or a week or two. For as long as I liked.

Wilfred pushed his chair back and stood up. "Which is my mother's room?"

I pointed down the stairs.

"Aiii!" Gladdy whispered, coming out of the kitchen when she heard him stamping down. "Big, big trouble down there!"

The front door opened and Tarquin came in, pushing Mohammed in a stroller. "Hello," he said, "where's Wilfred?" He was splotchy from the climb, and his coxcomb listed toward one ear. "Hello, Gladdy. Here's Mohammed."

Mohammed made a grab for the tassel of my dressing gown, and stuffed it into his mouth. But Tarquin came quickly around, squatting to uncurl the child's fingers and pry open his mouth. "Ow!" he cried, jumping up and holding out his finger. "The brat bit me!"

"Who bit who?" said Bess, traipsing into the chaos in her red silk kimono. "Ah, there's little Mustafa! Hello, boy! What's the matter?"

"He bit me!" Tarquin said. "He could have broken the skin!"

Wilfred bustled past her into the room, reaching down for the child. But as soon as he approached, Mohammed writhed and shrieked, holding his arms out desperately to Tarquin.

"Gladdy!" Wilfred shouted. "Would you kindly take this child for a walk?"

"Gladdy's nanny days are over," Bess said vaguely. "One should, perhaps, have remembered that ahead of time."

"Poisonous fucking bitch!" muttered Wilfred, splotchy himself now with fury.

Tarquin lifted the shrieking child from the stroller. "Wilfie," he said, "let's go!"

"Excellent idea!" said Bess.

"Indeed!" I added.

But this was too much for Wilfred. He wheeled around, narrowing his small eyes on me. "Stay out of this, you ridiculous old hag!" he hissed.

"Bess," I said carefully, "what's Dionysos's number?"

She looked at me, her eyes so wide and black and her hair so gorgeously disheveled that I could see quite easily how Finn had managed to overlook her bulk. "Here," she said, handing me her phone. "Just press three."

I took the phone into my room and closed the door, standing with my back against it for some seconds, waiting for my breathing to subside.

Was the year going to go on like this? I wondered. Lurching from one drama to the next until it was time to leave? They were shouting out there now, Gladdy's voice shriller even than Mohammed's. "GO!" she was shrieking. "YOU GO NOW FROM THIS HOUSE!"

So much, I thought, for the glorious peace of old age.

❧

à gg, Greece

Being called a ridiculous old hag by someone else's grown child is an entirely different experience from being called that or worse by one's own. The homegrown insult is generally a blunted instrument. Too many years of combat have gone into the blunting, and, willy-nilly, there will be more ahead. But "ridiculous old hag," hurled by a stranger who happens also to be Bess's nasty adult son? This has me standing before the mirror again, considering how easily the fragile triumphs of one's life can be diminished to nothing by a threadbare insult.

I peer more closely into it. *Ridiculous* old hag? Why do I even care about being thought a ridiculous old hag by a nasty little man who clearly can't stand women in the first place? Which, in his case, would be poor old Bess, who has the misfortune to be his mother.

So much of what has kept us feeling lucky here has been what I can only think of as a sort of springing, girlish hope. And much of this hope we seem to have accomplished without thought or intention, or even acknowledgment.

Or, at least, I have.

If, then, it can be dissolved so easily by a nasty insult, what can have been its value in the first place? And why, suddenly, considering all this, do I burst out laughing at the absurdity of it all?

☙

"WELL?" SAID BESS WHEN I handed back her phone.

"Dinny's coming. But what's the point if Wilfred has gone?"

"Oh, he'll be back," she said. "Wilfred has never been able to stand losing a fight."

Dania peered around her door. "The coast is clean?"

She came in and fell into a chair, arms and legs splayed as if she'd run a race. In the past few weeks she'd taken on a few more patients. They were begging her, she said, what could she do? "Maybe today I give to myself as a reward a baklava," she said.

"I ate the last one," I said quickly, in case she thought of blaming Bess. At least Wilfred's debit card had vanished from the table, I thought. At least that.

"Fur's back in," announced Bess from the window seat. "I mean real fur! Isn't that marvelous?"

Dania gave me the look, which, as usual, Bess caught. "But really," she insisted, "when you think of it, fake is always fake, I don't care how close it looks to the real thing."

"I love my fake coat," said Dania. "Also fleece. And you can wash it in the machine."

"How do you wash your shoes?" Bess said vaguely, turning the page. "You don't, do you? Gladdy cleans them. And brushes the furs."

Dania closed her eyes. She never allowed Gladdy to clean anything of hers, or even change her sheets. "I wouldn't scoop to that," she'd said to me.

There was a knock at the door, and in came Dionysos, trailing his customary cloud of cologne. Now that his wife was leaving us alone, we hardly remembered to lock it anymore, at least during the day.

"*Yasas!*" he said. "I come."

Bess climbed off the window seat and pattered over to him.

"You got trouble, Gina?" he said.

"My son," she whispered in the odd accent she affected with him. "He-ees-a-snake."

He kept his black eyes soberly on hers. "He at hotel, yes?"

She laughed merrily. "Is there anything you don't know about this island?"

"Agh!" said Dania, pushing herself to her feet. "The sun is out. Maybe I go to the bich."

"To the bitch, to the bitch!" sang Bess. "Let's all go to the bitch!"

But just as I was thinking that the beach wasn't a bad idea at all, the door opened again and back came Wilfred as Bess had predicted, with Tarquin behind him, and Mohammed chirruping in the stroller.

I watched Wilfred's glance flicker around the table, avoiding me, and settling finally on Dionysos. "Dr. Wilfred Saunderson," he said, walking around to him, holding out his hand.

I'd forgotten he was a doctor, it seemed so entirely improbable. And even though Bess had pointed out that he was only a dermatologist, still it was awful to think of him touching people with those small, white, fastidious fingers.

Dionysos took the hand deferentially, lifting himself slightly off his chair. "*Yasas*," he said.

Wilfred coughed a little, pulling a handkerchief out of his pocket and holding it to his nose.

"Ruthi?" said Dania, standing up. "You want to go to the bich?"

"Aii!" cried Bess. "Don't abandon me, Ruth!"

It was the sort of moment I was always trying to avoid— having to choose between them. But Dania wasn't waiting for my answer. She walked off to her room, returning after a few minutes with a beach towel and the black portmanteau she carried everywhere. "I'll take the car," she said. "I have with me my phone. Maybe you can ask Dionysos to bring you there in his car."

Again Wilfred flapped the handkerchief. "Whew!" he coughed as soon as she'd gone. "What is it our Golda Meir has doused herself in? Sheep dip?"

"Wilfred," said Bess. "Where is Turkey? Mustafa is climbing into the spa."

◉

Ruth, dear, Amy's come up with an idea! Considering the responses
we've been getting to the more snarky offerings, how would you feel
if we changed the name of the column to "Don't Get Me Started"?
Don't you think it fits the sort of edgy feel you're so good at? I know
this isn't what we'd agreed on to start with, but what do you think?
We think it could be a wow. It doesn't mean, of course, that we don't
want recipes, etc. The readers adore them! If you shoot me a quick
response, we'll get started on the layout ASAP. Sxx

◉

Good idea, Stacey. In fact, a relief. I append the latest under the new
rubric. A bit low on snark, though. So, maybe you'd like to hold off
until the next? Ruth

◉

DGMS, Greece
The Mediterranean diet has been receiving a lot of press lately,
especially in places like London and New York. But what the zealots
of the you-are-what-you-eat brigade don't seem to understand is the
life that goes with the diet—the long-established habits and associations,
the rhythms, the priorities that don't include a Pilates class or even
divorce court.

On the island of Ikaria, for instance, inhabitants, renowned for their
longevity, sleep late, work hard, take long naps, make love until they die,
die long after the age of ninety, spend lots of time before they do with
friends, drink goat's milk, coffee, wine, a tea made of wild herbs, and eat
mostly beans, greens, potatoes, olive oil, and honey. The island has
become famous for its style of life since one of its inhabitants—having

emigrated as a young man to America, contracted cancer there, and been given six months to live—returned to his parents' home to die. And lived on there for another thirty-six years, outlasting even his American doctors.

We had read about this man before we arrived in Greece and thought we might have a go at his style of life. But we failed almost from the start. How, for instance, do you force yourself to stay asleep until 11 a.m.? Or to fall asleep in the first place when, night after night, you are in a fight to the death with insomnia? Even if I try an afternoon nap, I just lie there, wide awake, thinking of how much I'd rather be swimming, or walking, or just sitting at the edge of the veranda as we did after lunch today, all of us talking about home, and the way we have freed ourselves from the strictures and habits of the worlds we came from, so that, wherever we are, we've managed to be at home in our lives away from home. Here, there, anywhere.

❧

WE ALL ENDED UP GOING to the beach, even Gladdy. There she was, down at the water's edge, her skirt hitched up, collecting seawater in the bottle she'd brought along. It is for her bowels, Bess explained, an old African remedy.

"Remedy for what?" said Dania.

"Oh, God," Bess muttered, laying her head on Dionysos's thigh as if there were no reason in the world not to. "For the sorrow that cannot speak its name."

"Constipation," I explained.

Dionysos was pretending to concentrate on Gladdy, but I could see from the way his hand kept straying from its resting place on the towel that he was longing to stroke Bess's hair or touch her face. As it was, he just stared dreamily down toward the water while the three of us became animated on the subject of bowels.

"I mean, what about when you're with a new lover?" said Bess.

"I was once almost ten days in the Seychelles before, at last, the sorrow came to an end."

"Sometimes it's the men who are neurotic like that," said Dania. "Amos was very neurotic about it. No one could be even outside the door to hear him."

But mention of Amos killed the fun, even for Bess, who didn't know the full story.

"No skin from my teeth," Dania said. "I don't have in life this problem, thanks Gott."

꩜

JUST BEFORE DANIA MARRIED AMOS, a woman had phoned her. "If you want to hear things about Amos," she'd said, "meet me tomorrow and I'll tell you."

So Dania had gone to meet the woman. She found her sitting in a dark corner of the café, a woman she recognized from the bank—young and sexy and cheaply dressed. On the table in front of her was a small tape recorder.

As soon as Dania was seated, the young woman switched it on. And from it came Amos's voice—Amos saying things about her, about Dania—things so intimate, so private, so stinging, and so heartless that all she could do when it was over was to pick up her bag and leave the café.

"I had today from a woman who works in the bank a phone call about you," she told Amos when he came home. "Tomorrow she wants to meet me, to tell me what she knows."

Amos had to sit down in his agitation. "That woman from the bank?" he said. "She's crazy! Don't bother to go!"

"Crazy I understand," said Dania quite calmly.

"Listen," he said, "she threw herself at me. What could I do? You were away, you were gone for months."

Dania gave him her bloodless smile.

"So, yes, okay," he said, "okay, I went to her apartment once after work. But only once. Not even for the whole night."

"Sit down!" Dania barked because, in his agitation, he'd sprung up and was actually tearing at his hair.

He sat down like a mouse. "It will never happen again," he said in a small voice. "Never. I can promise you that. One night. It was nothing. She's nothing to me."

And that's when Dania told him the truth. Not only did she know the affair had been going on for two years, but she'd heard the complaints he'd made about her—complaints about her, Dr. Dania Weiss, who was paying the bills and building the house—heard him say to this cheap little *bank teller* that *she* was not *attractive* to him. She was too *old*? Too *wrinkled*? To this *bank teller*? TO THIS RUBBISH YEMENI BANK TELLER!?

She'd lowered her voice then and stared at him while he squirmed and cried. "If it happens again," she'd said, barely audible now, "if *ever* it happens again, you should know this: I. WILL. KILL. YOU!"

❧

WHEN SHE'D TOLD ME ALL THIS—delivering the final sentence in the low voice of menace I'd heard her use once on a window cleaner who'd left smears across the glass—I'd stared at her, staggering suddenly under the burden of all the years of exulting I'd endured from her—the perfect life, the perfect lovers, and now this perfect Amos squirming like a mouse under his sentence of death. And the wonder of it was that, quite soon afterward, she forgot she'd ever told me. "Look it, Ruthi," she said. "I've got everything I want! Wonderful house! Wonderful job! Wonderful husband!"

◉

Ruth, dear, we're holding off on DGMS after all. Amy's having second thoughts. So, back to our grannies, at least till further notice! Go for it! Sxx

◉

à gg, Greece

Dania is as good at sleeping through the night as she is at hole-in-the-floor toilet. And she disapproves greatly of Bess's cornucopia of sleeping pills. Still, without those pills—and, for me, my more modest supply—both Bess and I would be good for nothing after a night of no sleep. Bess is no good at falling asleep, and I'm no good at staying asleep. So Bess doses up a good hour before going to bed, lining the pills up along the edge of her bathroom shelf. And then, within ten minutes or so, off she goes, and one can hear the snoring even one floor up.

Sleep apnea, Dania pronounces with authority. Bess should go to a clinic, she says, and get one of those breathing machines.

I know a number of women who use those machines and, not incidentally, end up with a bedroom to themselves. Who, after all, can sleep with a lawn mower running? How, in fact, do the sleepers themselves manage? I suppose, once you're hooked, you're hooked, even to a lawn mower. As I see it, these apnerians are as hooked on their machines as Bess is on her pills.

Meanwhile, except for people like Dania and the Ikarians, the night can spell real misery for grannies without machines or pills. Even the sight of a pillow—silent, blameless, defiant—can bring on dread. In she climbs anyway—after all, what's the alternative?—lies down, puts on her glasses, picks up her book. At least she knows she has one of

Bess's little helpers just in case. It's cut into quarters and sitting in a saucer in the bathroom. So when, ten or thirty or even sixty minutes after falling asleep, she jumps awake again—light still on, glasses down her nose, book facedown, and heart galloping—there's hope that she'll survive another night of it.

☉

JUST AS WE WERE GATHERING up our things to climb the hill to the car, Wilfred came down, carrying a large, covered basket, Tarquin following with Mohammed.

"Mohammed came to the mountain," Bess murmured. "Hello," she said to Wilfred, "we're just leaving."

"We changed our plans," he said. "Mohammed had to have a sleep."

She chucked the child under the chin, and he lifted his hand to touch the skin she had touched, staring shyly at her from under his lovely, curling lashes.

"Where shall we have lunch?" she said, turning to me.

But I saw the child watching her, baffled, and suddenly I longed for her to turn and scoop him into her arms, kiss his neck, make him laugh.

"We brought lunch for everyone," Wilfred said quickly. "The hotel scrambled it together." He pretended not to be asking, but clearly there was an invitation in the studied casualness of his voice.

"I loathe picnics," said Bess. "And, anyway, the wind is going to start up any minute."

I put my bag down. Never mind that Mohammed wasn't his, it was as if I were seeing Wilfred in the child, his mother so deeply uninterested in his existence that there was nothing he could do to have her decide he might be worth the trouble of having lunch with. "I'll take him," I said, "if he doesn't object."

Gladdy looked up when I reached the water's edge. "Hau, Ruthi, you the nanny now?"

Mohammed strained and jumped in my arms, wanting to be free to plunge into the water.

"Hang on, hang on," I said, putting him down on the stones. But immediately he began to clamber toward the surf.

"Hai, Ruthi!" Gladdy said, hauling herself to her feet. "No more peace now!" She grasped the child expertly under his arms and plonked him between her knees, holding him in place there. "Here," she said to him, "you play with some stones."

He turned to look at her with the same puzzled stare he'd given Bess. And again I wished to see him scooped up and properly loved. Once, when I'd swung Hester into the air as an infant, and she'd rolled into a laugh, a real laugh, I'd grabbed her into my arms and kissed her fiercely, understanding, suddenly, the joy women were supposed to feel in their babies, and of which, until then, I had been so bereft.

So, perhaps, I thought now, this child, saddled as he was with such fathers and with his improbable name—perhaps he just needed someone to love him properly, someone to whom he'd belong more truly than he ever could to Wilfred and Tarquin.

"Lunch in five minutes!" Wilfred called down.

"What lunch?" said Gladdy.

"For all of us," I said. "They brought it from the hotel."

She brushed some sand from Mohammed's hair. "What they going to do when this boy he grows too big?"

I shrugged.

"That's what I told Wilfie. What happens when the child he asks for his own people?"

The child himself was now happily piling stones onto Gladdy's thigh and then knocking them off.

"Well, what is going to happen?" I asked.

"The child he's going to blame Wilfie."

"But children blame us anyway," I said, remembering Patience sitting grimly in the wicker chair.

She shrugged. "They are blaming their own parents. This boy he's going to blame Wilfie. Wilfie is not a parent."

I sat up. "Is it Wilfred you're worried about then, or the child?"

But she just closed her lips at this, one hand still toying with a stone.

"Lunch!" Tarquin shouted. "Ruth! Gladdy!"

Gladdy handed Mohammed to me to carry back up to the picnic. I'd heard of animals behaving like this in the bush— shooing off a strange cub or calf to starve or be eaten. Or killing it themselves if they could.

"Here," I said to Tarquin, handing Mohammed over just as he began to yell. Bowls of melitzanosalata and tzatziki had been laid out, platters of spanakopita, meatballs, tiropitas, and two bottles of wine.

"Where's Dania?" I said. "Where's Bess?"

"Gone," sang Wilfred. "And Aristophanes with them. How about a glass of wine, Ruth?" he said. "Gladdy? We brought you a beer, comme d'hab."

And so there we sat, an odd arrangement, with Gladdy leaning against the tree, drinking her beer from the bottle, Tarquin feeding Mohammed from a jar, and Wilfred and me with glasses of wine, facing out to sea.

"I've read two of your books, you know," he said suddenly.

Here we go, I thought.

"That detective of yours—Steven Grim—Tarquin!" he snapped, turning around. "Can you please stop him whining?"

"Gripp," I murmured. "Stefan Gripp."

"But I meant to ask you," he said, turning back, "why the war? Why not now, say?"

I shrugged. The last thing I wanted was to be pulled into a discussion of my literary choices with Wilfred.

He gave my knee a pat. "Did you ever read that book about a group of women who meet to peel potatoes? On one of the Channel Islands? Also set during the war? No? Well, you might consider it," he said. "It really is quite amusing."

☙

à gg, Greece

Bess here again. This morning I asked Ruth and Dania why they've given up on romance.

They laughed. They often laugh when I ask things like that. Then Ruth said it was because she was sick of listening to men talk about themselves, and Dania said she gets paid to listen to people talk about themselves, so why should she listen for nothing?

Why listen to any of them? I asked. Why not just *pretend* to listen while you look at their hands?

Hands? they said.

But then Ruth said, In fact—she's always saying "in fact"—she loves large, muscular, masterful hands in a man, sinewy and tanned, with a great wide grasp like the ones her old lover had, the one who was murdered. (Finn, her last lover, says the memory of that man is hard to live with—like competing with Jesus, Mary, and Joseph all rolled into one.)

Okay, I said, so what about wine?

Well, Dania hardly drinks, and clearly she thinks she doesn't need wine for romance or for anything else either.

But really, I said, is there anything less romantic than a man who doesn't drink? He's going to be a prig, or an ex-alcoholic just waiting for you to be drunk enough to push into bed.

Oh, bed! said Dania. Agh, the sagging body.

Well, who wants to see *their* sagging bodies? said Ruth, up in arms. Who wants to keep boosting *their* sagging morales? Who wants any of the sad, played-out old farce anymore? (That's the way she talks.)

But the bodies aren't even the *point*! I shouted, because Ruth's furies can be quite catchy—it's the *idea* of the bodies! Just look at Dinny and me. We're fat, he has small, white, hairy fingers, and he even wears a truss. But when we sit across a table, laughing and eating and making our way through a second carafe of wine, who could think of anything but how lovely it all is?

☙

BY THE TIME WILFRED AND family left the island, the three of us had sorted out Bess's finances. What we decided was that we would revert to dividing things into thirds, never mind Gladdy, who, after all, had never even been paid for what she did for us. Dania and I would split the costs until Bess's funds arrived from South Africa, and no one would tell Gladdy any of this. She was not to be trusted, said Bess, she'd just go and tell Wilfred or Agnes, and then they'd hear about the money from

South Africa and suspend the measly debit card they were allowing her.

"As if I didn't buy them each a house!" she cried. "As if their father didn't set both of them up with *trust* funds! With *my* money!" She huffed down on the pillows. "I told him it was a stupid idea, but, oh no, he said, we were a 'family'—he loved that word—and he wanted to do for them what had never been done for him. Well, of course it hadn't been done for him—his mother killed herself when he was twelve and his father took up with the housekeeper. Men and money!" she said. "You should write a column about *that*, Ruth!"

Actually, it was a fine idea, balancing the one about women and money. And if I could think of a way to bring in Dania, Amos, and Wendy, there'd be a few columns' worth. Except, of course, that Dania would never agree. And I still suffered the odd dog-in-the-manger-ish surge of resentment against Bess for snatching Finn from me.

⌾

Ruth, dear, Amy likes this last piece a lot (romance, men's hands, etc.). But it really needs shaping. And could you please have Bess play down the alcohol? As you know, we've been devoting a lot of copy to breast cancer, and alcohol is one big no-no. Amy says the Ikarians must be okay because their wine is organic. Do you think you could talk Bess into substituting, say, candy for alcohol? Valentine's Day, etc.? :) I gather you're back on speaking terms? Frankly, I'd rather not have another go-round with her myself. Sxx

⌾

"CANDY?" CRIED BESS. "Is she *serious*!" She stomped off to the kitchen, and was soon back with two glasses of her favorite

Sancerre, bought at great cost from the wine shop down at the port. She handed one to me. "Listen," she said, taking a slug, "just tell that New York cow from me that she can take a running jump. *Candy*, for God's sake! *Organic!* I *ask* you!"

☙

BESS AND I WERE BACK on speaking terms. More than speaking terms, we'd even begun to laugh about Finn. And she'd picked up again with Dionysos, although it wasn't clear whether the romance was back on, too. From time to time, they would drive off together, presumably when the wife was on another island. And then back she would come earlier than usual with stories of a baptism or a wedding and, oh, God, the lascivious priests! Her money had arrived at last as well, and so now she had her own debit card and insisted on paying us everything she'd owed. She would have paid more than she owed had we not loudly refused to take it.

"Shhh!" she'd hissed then, gesticulating toward the kitchen.

Dania threw up her hands. "But how does she think you are buying again those clothes?" she whispered. "It is impossible she doesn't know."

She had a point. Bess was shopping again at the old pace. She'd even found a small shop that specialized in the sort of overpriced Riviera-esque clothing she favored, and the French owner kept leaving messages with Gladdy—the sandals Bess wanted had come in, or a caftan, or a blouse.

"Wouldn't it be better," I said, "just to tell her?"

Bess huffed. She hadn't forgiven Gladdy for summoning Wilfred, and Gladdy herself was huffing around in response.

Meanwhile, the sun was warmer day to day, and we were all warming up with it. Even Dania found it in her to say she was pleased Wilfred had failed to bring Bess to her knees. "Thanks Gott, Ruthi," she said, "we don't have such a son!"

"I don't have any son period," I said. "If I did, maybe he'd behave better than our daughters."

A few days before, Yael had announced that she wouldn't be coming in June after all. What she and the children wanted, she'd said, was the sort of time they'd had with Dania when they'd come at Christmas. What she certainly didn't want was to be shacked up with strangers and strange children, birthday or no birthday. In fact, she'd far prefer to spend her holiday some-where *she* chose to be, which wouldn't be with strangers, etc. So, what about Santorini? she said. In fact, she'd already found a house to rent right down on the water, with the use of a yacht thrown in. Perhaps Dania would visit them *there* for her birthday? At least for a day or so? She'd have to share with the children, there were only two bedrooms, but she'd have her days to herself unless she wanted to go sailing with them.

"The nerves of her!" said Dania, closing her laptop. "First I must give the money for the new guest room, and now she rents for herself a yught!"

"Daniushka!" I said. "You didn't shell out *again*?"

"Again what?" said Bess from her perch.

"Agh," said Dania. "I give, I give, she's snotty and superior."

"But I thought she was a doctor?" said Bess.

"Research doctor," said Dania. "Still, she makes with the job more than I do. If you ask me, we're all crazy."

I could see that, birthday or no birthday, the rejection had wounded her, and that money had little to do with it. Yael had unsettled her image of herself as mother and grandmother, just as Amos had unsettled her image as woman and wife. All she was left with, in the ongoing performance of her life, was the one member of the audience whose applause she'd always been able to count on, even ten or twenty years after his death: her father. "Ruthi," she'd say, "for him I was always a star, never mind he was a narcissist." As I saw it, it was for him she still boasted so insistently because, unless she could keep fueling the great boastful pride he had always had in her, not only could she not count her life a triumph, but she, Dania Weiss, about to enter her eighth decade, would be, as she would put it, an orphant.

☙

à gg, Greece

Two of the children have staged a takeover. The excuse for this is our seventieth birthdays—Dania's and mine in June; Bess's and Gladdy's in September—never mind that none of us wants a celebration, and certainly not one we'll have to arrange ourselves.

We talk a lot about how to escape (yet again), but none of us, except Bess, seems to have the courage to refuse her children on this one. One might consider this charming—not wanting to disappoint the children—but the truth is that it's not their disappointment we fear; it's *them*. Or them *in* their disappointment. Or something.

So, what is it about this game of parent-and-child that has us playing the version of ourselves that our adult children have chosen for us? The only one, as I say, who has managed to resist this charade is Bess, and then only with her son. With him she's offhand, careless, a sort of wayward aunt. But with her daughter she can turn into a child herself, flapping about and asking for help when clearly she doesn't need it. Perhaps she does this without thinking—wanting to give her life-coaching daughter something to coach in her.

Who knows? And who knows why Dania, at her daughter's half-hearted invitation, is planning to celebrate her own birthday ahead of time on a different island? A trip involving almost a day's travel on ferries and no small outlay of money? Because she would feel worse saying no?

And what about me? Unable to tell Hester that this celebration is anathema to me—anathema to Bess as well—never mind the habit of frankness I've always prided myself on with her? Quite uncharacteristically, I've been conducting sideways maneuvers—suggesting postponements, alternatives, lies, lies, lies—and then pretending to laugh along when she says, You're not getting out of this one, Mum! Just like the tyrant she is.

The only one of us who doesn't object to the takeover is Gladdy. She will bake a cake, she says, and invite her Greek friends, even the ponytailed priest. Apparently, he no longer terrifies her. She waves when she passes him on the street, a shy little schoolgirl's wave, and he nods back with a benignant smile.

☉

Ruth, dear, thank goodness we held off on DGMS. We did a reader survey, and they LOVE "à Go Go." It makes them laugh, even the snarky ones. :) So should we just call it an experiment that failed? Sxx

☉

ONE DAY, OUT OF THE BLUE, in walked Rex, and there he stood where they all stood the first time they came into the house, just beyond the threshold, gazing out through the glass doors, down toward the Aegean. "Beautiful," he murmured, Panama in hand. And even Dania seemed to wake up at the sight of him.

"Ruth?" he said. "You must be Ruth." He held out his hand. "I recognize you from your book photograph."

I flushed, I couldn't help it. He was a tall, tanned, beautifully symmetrical man with deep blue eyes, a graying head of thick wavy hair, and the slightly bemused look of a cultured and worldly European. Standing there, my hand still in his, I understood quite suddenly, and with the sort of sobriety generally brought to bear on terminal illness, that, seventy or not, I could count on no end to the sort of awkwardness that, even now, had taken over my power of speech.

"And I am Dania," announced Dania from her customary chair.

He went over to shake her hand. Soon she would be excusing herself to take the first of her morning phone calls. Gladdy was down at the shops, Bess wouldn't wake for another hour at least and, oh, God, what was I going to do with him?

"Do you have luggage?" I said, sitting on the couch.

"Left it down at the hotel," he said, settling himself at the other end. "Charming room, with a view of those beautiful dovecotes they build here. The whole flock seems to leave and return together. But it's nothing like your view up here. Isn't this just heavenly!" He sat back and stretched out his long legs, quite comfortable, apparently, with the space and time he was taking up.

"Gladdy's friends tried to teach her to make stuffed pigeon," I offered, "but she won't hear of it."

"Ah, Gladdy!" He smiled. "Where's the old Cerberus?"

I laughed. What was it to me that he'd lost Bess's money? Or even that he'd turned his back on a pregnant au pair? In fact, I almost envied the au pair her fecundity.

Dania looked at her watch. "I have in my room an appointment," she announced, standing up.

He leapt to his feet. "Perhaps you'll all dine with me to-night? At the hotel? Or anywhere you choose. I feel as if I know you both already from Bess's e-mails."

So Bess had been e-mailing him? I wasn't really surprised. What did surprise me was the man himself. If I'd written him into a Gripp novel, he'd have been the victim—too decent, too superior in his views of human nature to have seen it coming. Or too much in love with the spy herself to resist being veered off course.

"Does Bess know you're here?" I asked casually.

He laughed. "I sail these islands every May. This year it'll be the Turquoise Coast."

"Oh, I see."

But I didn't see, of course. Where was the Turquoise Coast? And would he be carrying Bess off with him? Anything seemed possible.

Outside, the fish man began his wail and the church bells started up, setting the dogs howling.

"Ah Greece!" he said, smiling out again through the glass doors. No man except Hugh had ever shocked me into this sort of attention, never mind how beautiful he happened to be. Usually, if there was an appeal, it arrived with the game of conversation. But here was Rex, quite comfortable with silence. And so, watching him, I settled comfortably into it myself.

And then suddenly he leaned forward. "Bess doesn't know this," he said, "but Irina's child will probably be born this week or next. That's why I slipped away early."

"The au pair?"

He nodded. "I asked her to have a DNA test, you know."

Apparently, this was a question. But before I could think

of an answer, he said, "Were the child mine, she would surely have agreed, wouldn't you think?"

I longed to look at my watch. It could be another hour before Bess emerged to bring this to an end.

"The fact is, I'm unable to have a child," he said. "Bess knows this, and Irina knew it, too."

"And if it is yours?" I said quickly. "Such things do happen."

He shrugged. "Were the child mine, I'd believe in a god. Believe me, I would."

              ◎

Hester #5

Talking to Rex about the baby he's so hoping is his, I couldn't help thinking back to the birth of Hester—how young I was then, how cut adrift by Hugh's murder. And then of Lily as a newborn, folded under Hester's arm or laid across her opulent body. How happy Hester was with her there—how complete, uncomplicated, triumphant. Watching them, I understood for the first time what she had missed with me. And I was sorry for both of us, sorry for myself never to have been trapped like her in that desperate bond, made irrational by it, one-eyed, devious, homicidal.

              ◎

DINNER AT THE HOTEL WAS like a celebration. We sat at a long table outside, under the trellis, a brazier burning at either end against the chill. Bess had insisted on asking Dionysos to join us, and so there he sat at the foot of the table, between her and Gladdy, ordering, offering, overseeing food and wine as if he himself were the host.

Which, as it turned out, he was. And then off he went with Bess, leaving Rex to watch them go.

"What did you think?" said Dania as we climbed the hill afterward to the village.

"Of Rex?"

"Of course of him. Ruthi! How long have we known each other?"

We often asked each other this, although we both knew perfectly well it had been more than forty years.

"I don't know what to believe about him," I said. "Or who."

"Just be careful," she said. "He's got a mean face."

"What?" I stopped where I was. "The man's a beauty!"

She shrugged. "What can I do, you like mean-looking men? It's because of your father."

"My father!" All these years I'd stopped short of telling her what I really thought of the men in her life, including her own tiresome, boastful father.

But, before I could find a way to tell her this now, she'd stretched out her arms and was touching her toes. "Thanks Gott I do my exercises every morning," she said. "Who would believe it? Seventy, and I'm still climbing mountains!"

"Seventy," I said, "and still boasting."

She cocked her head at me, and then threw it back and guffawed. "Oh, Ruthi!" she cried. "We have to learn each of us a lesson in silence before the next birthday!"

☙

à gg, Greece

As the year progresses, I've been thinking more and more of how differently our various backgrounds persist in fashioning the way we are as adults. Bess and I, for instance: having both grown up in what was once part of a great empire—savage in its self-justifications, relentless in pursuit of its own interests—I learned very early not to try to answer the furious question, so antithetical to the idea of empire itself, that lay at the heart of its strict code of conduct: *Who do you think you are?*

One didn't answer this, of course, because one knew it was simply a lesson in humility: in the eyes of that world one was nothing—a pebble on the beach, a brick in the wall. Privately, one might consider oneself hot stuff—invaluable to the family, the society, the world, the universe, and so forth—but in one's public demeanor one was to be nothing more than that pebble or that brick.

And yet Bess, who grew up in the same place, if not the same society as I, never seems to have cottoned to the public/private aspect of the who-do-you-think-you-are question. She tends to embrace the whole idea of being nothing more than that pebble or that brick—uses it quite often, in fact, saying, Who am I to decide? And then, somehow, managing to decide for herself anyway, doing just as she pleases.

At the other end of the spectre, as Dania would say, is Dania herself. Who-do-you-think-you-are had no part in the world in which she grew up. There, each child was a triumph over the murderous fury and rage of the Germans, the indifference of the world. I tell myself this when her boasting, yet again, gets out of hand. Or when, as fed up as the rest of us by children, she will admit to this only in a whisper. It is as if she considers the admission as shocking as I would my own were I to boast to her, or to anyone, that, come to think of it, I really was hot stuff.

Which, I should add, I most certainly am not.

☙

I TRIED TO ENVISAGE REX as the sort of harebrained dreamer who would lose a woman her fortune but, with the man actually before me, it was impossible. When I'd asked Bess how he'd done it, she'd just thrown up her hands. "Honestly," she said, "I don't know. He seemed to lose it lump by lump, and then suddenly there were no lumps left."

"Like on what?"

She stretched back against the pillows. "Like the silk lampshades he was going to make a fortune on. Trips to India first class—and who knows who he took with him? Certainly wasn't me. I mean, who ever thought of losing money on lampshades?"

I shrugged. "It doesn't seem to fit."

"Well, you'd better watch out. Next thing he'll be carrying you off on a yacht and then suddenly you'll be on your beam ends like me."

"At least I wouldn't be pregnant."

She laughed. If she'd been like a violent Greek wife over the au pair, she certainly wasn't anymore. Day after day Rex strolled in, settled himself next to me, and fell into the sort of talk that couldn't possibly interest her. Stefan Gripp, for instance. What had made me think of having him play Bach when he had to think through a case? Rex wanted to know. Surely I must play myself? How else could I possibly have described so accurately the satisfaction of playing Bach for oneself, even poorly? The way it focuses the mind and settles the spirit?

"Ruthi is a very good pianist!" Dania announced.

"Oh, for God's sake!" I said. Apart from the fact that Dania had never heard me play—apart from the fact that I hadn't played for years, decades, and even then had never amounted to much—she was damned, I could see, if she was going to let this mean-faced man leap the forty years she and I had shared and into the sort of intimacy that had me, for once, agreeing to discuss Stefan Gripp.

"Why did you kill him off then?" he asked, ignoring her.

"She was probably sick of him," Bess said. She lowered her magazine and looked at him over the top of her glasses. "Women can get quite sick of knowing what's coming next, you know."

It was the first sign of sharpness she'd shown toward him.

"But that was the trouble," I said. "I *didn't* know and, as a matter of fact, I got quite sick of the struggle to find out."

She snapped the magazine back into place with a snort, and he lifted his eyebrows. I didn't join in, I didn't need to. For the first time in twenty or thirty years, the triumph of routing a rival was sweeping over me. How on earth had I endured the way she'd swept Finn off for herself? And then sauntered back again when Wilfred turned up, trying to make a joke of it all? Well, here I was, and here was Rex suggesting *sotto voce* that perhaps I'd show him round the island before he took off.

My phone binged—another urgent text from Stacey, for God's sake. "How would now do?" I said. "I'll just grab my bag and we can slip out."

☙

BUT, CLOSED INTO THE CAR with him, I was suddenly mute as a teenager. "I was wondering," he was saying, "how you'd get away from the two of them. But then there you were, sailing right out like Athena."

I stared soberly ahead, negotiating a curve. *Athena, for God's sake!*

"Ah!" he said, rolling down his window. "Greece!"

But nothing he could say now seemed able to elicit from me more than a nod. And so, as if to balance things, he began to wax voluble himself. How did we make it work, he wanted to know, three such different women in such close quarters? And what was Dania's story? How did she cope with Gladdy? And what about Dionysos? Poor sod didn't have a chance once Bess had set her sights on him, did he?

I stepped on the accelerator, plunging us downhill. With him grilling me like this, the outing didn't seem like such a good idea anymore. Ridiculous as it was, I was missing the others, even Bess. Up there, with her looking on, talking to him had been easy. But here, locked into the car, I wanted only to find a way to shut him up.

I squealed around the bends, slamming on the brakes, swerving to avoid oncoming cars.

"Jesus!" he said when we came to a stop at the restaurant. "Do you always drive like that?"

I smiled, restored a bit by his fright. "I love this place," I said. "I don't know why I don't come down here more often."

"Well, if you don't plunge us off a cliff on the way, why don't we come back tomorrow? I leave on Friday, you know."

I chose a table right at the edge of the dock. It was the first time since September that I'd come down here, and the umbrellas were out again, the cats and the kittens, and the fishing boats tied up in the heat of the day.

"Actually," I said, "I'm generally quite a sober driver."

"Well, you've managed to drive me to alcohol." He settled back into his sardonic smile. "Shall I order us some wine? Red? White? Both?"

"Both," I said. Wine, I thought, might restore me to myself. Clearly, there was no understanding this at any age.

"I think they have the right idea here with their siestas," he said. "Don't you?"

"God, no! If I slept all afternoon I'd sleep even less at night."

But he was busy with the waitress now—ordering, consulting, ordering some more. "Insomnia?" he said vaguely, turning back to me. "You don't look like the sort! Do you take pills for it? Like Bess?"

Ah, Bess again.

"I forgot to ask whether you'd rather have ouzo," he said.

"No ouzo, thanks." Why, I wondered, were we still finding it so difficult to land on normal conversation?

"It's always been an ambition of mine to learn to like ouzo. Or even grappa, though grappa is worse, I think."

"I learned early to like ouzo," I said. "There are better and worse versions, of course, and one is always being told one hasn't tasted the right sort. We have some ouzo at the house. You could test your ambition there."

"I'm not sure Cerberus would appreciate my spitting it out into her sink."

"I've been considering a column on ambition," I said quickly, "how it tends to lift with age. Don't you find that?"

The truth was that, until that moment, I'd been considering no such thing. And, now that I did, I saw that the lifting applied only to me. Dania, whatever she said, counted on commanding the summit or, at least, being seen to command it. And Bess, a complete stranger to ambition, couldn't see the point of it at all, either in man or woman.

I looked over at him for an answer, but he was staring at a yacht coming into the harbor. His mouth hung open slightly, and then drew itself into the sort of apprising smile of a practiced roué. It was something that would have had me standing up to leave were he Finn, and the yacht, indeed, another woman. But he wasn't Finn, and I reached over for the carafe, rather wishing that he were.

"Oh, do forgive me!" he said, spinning around. "I was captivated by that gorgeous creature out there! What is it you were asking?"

I smiled indulgently.

"I'd give anything to sail something like that," he said, shaking his head. "But, whoo, I'm under the whip hand now."

I looked at him, this man who seemed to bring all subjects back to Bess. "How was the money lost?" I said. What are you living on now? I wanted to know. And who will be paying for lunch?

He stretched back in his chair. "It wasn't I who spent it, my dear, it was she. Granted, she spent it on both of us—handed over control, in fact. All her other men, you see, had paid the bills themselves, one way or another. Had I been another man, I would have stepped in and stopped her. But I'm not another man, you see, so I rather gave myself over to her extravagance. And then came the coup de grâce with the au pair."

"And the lampshades?"

"Oh that. Oh yes. That, I admit, was a mistake. I had an Indian mistress, you see, so the lampshades were really just an excuse."

Despite myself, I felt my blood rising on Bess's behalf, or on my own, it was hard to tell which. "Other mistresses as well?"

He laughed. "An insuperable weakness of mine," he said.

And he reached over for my hand.

❧

Ruth, dear, Amy thinks the piece on empire, etc., might be perfect for, say, a literary quarterly, but for our readership she wants a little more of that Greek sunshine :) Or even snark :) Those recipes you promised? Soon? We're closing, like, now! Sxx

à gg, Greece
Many of you have written to ask how we decided to divide up our daily tasks and chores once Gladdy joined us here. All I can say is that we all, including Gladdy, seem to have come to an unspoken accord in the matter.

Take cooking, for instance. Unless we go to a restaurant, Gladdy cooks our meals. In itself, this is no hardship as she's a marvelous plain cook. But she's also bossy, and has idiosyncratic standards that preclude, for instance, gyros. So, if we want a gyro, we are reduced to creeping out to get one when she isn't looking. She disapproves of gyros from the corner shop. And she disapproves of restaurants, which, as she terms it, are "essravaguss."

Why, one may well ask, does one care what she approves or disapproves of? But this would be to ignore the fact that she refuses to consider herself an employee. Nor will she agree to be paid as one. What she will accept is a gift of money every week, which, we are to understand, is a present, not a wage. What's wrong with earning a wage? Well, if she earned a wage, says she, she would have to do what we told her to do, and this doesn't suit her.

The trouble is that if things don't go her way, she can make life pretty awful. First, she won't hear you when you speak to her, and then, if you put yourself in front of her, she won't see you either.

All this has made me vow never again to agree to an arrangement in which, if services are rendered, they are not properly contracted and paid for. Bess says Gladdy has always been this way, even when she first came to London for the birth of Agnes, Bess's daughter. And anyway, she said, Gladdy has accumulated a far larger fortune with her weekly "presents" than she would have done had she had to pay taxes. She keeps her stash in the bank, says Bess. And except for the times she's had to shell out to her own daughter or grandson, she's been frugal beyond imagining and could probably buy and sell us all a few times over by now. Which wouldn't be too difficult when it came to Bess herself, now that she's cheap on the market.

❋

ALL THE WAY BACK UP the hill, I thanked God for the waning of desire. Twenty or even ten years earlier, I wouldn't have tried to talk myself out of stopping with him at the hotel, as he was now asking me to do, so awful would have been my terror of regret if I did not. The offer ("What about trying out a siesta at the hotel?") was rather low in desire itself, and my laughing refusal seemed to put an easy end to it.

Anyway, I already felt as if I'd betrayed them all, Gladdy included, just by going off with him. What would I tell them when I returned? How could I just saunter back in as if nothing had happened? Especially when nothing really had happened?

But then, when we reached the hotel, he turned to me quite soberly and said, "Ruth, could you bear to come in with me?"

"That's not the right question," I said, parrying for time. But, oh God, with his soft voice and puzzled frown the old terror of regret was, indeed, taking hold of me.

"We could just lie there and listen to the pigeons," he said, smiling.

At least, I thought, he isn't stupid enough to say, "We're neither of us children, my dear." Still, the fact hung between us unsaid, making an absurdity of my reluctance.

I switched off the car and climbed out.

"Look," I said as soon as we were closed into his room. "For every sort of reason I think this is a mistake—"

He held up a hand. "Give me a minute," he said. Then he disappeared into the bathroom.

This sort of situation, I thought, must be habitual with him. And yet to dash off now like a child would be ridiculous. On the other hand, to stay and opt for listening to pigeons? I walked onto the balcony to look at them and, yes, there they were, cooing along the ledges, and then, suddenly, the whole flock of them swooping out and down into the valley. The fact was, I decided, there really was nothing romantic about two adults around seventy in a hotel room, never mind the Ikarians or the glamorized ads in cruise brochures. Sex made most sense when it was at its most thoughtless, most urgent, most dangerous. And when it carried with it the chance of a child.

Perhaps, I thought, cheering up, I'll do a column on that, although Amy will doubtless want the LGBT-etc. crowd included, which would make nonsense of the whole idea—

And that's when he came up behind me, smelling of soap and toothpaste, and took me by the shoulders. Thank God, I thought, turning to face him—thank God Gripp is dead and never, not in this life or the next, will I have to write another sex scene.

⟡

WHEN I WALKED BACK INTO the house, it was as if into a hold-up. There, in the middle of the room, stood a tall, bleached, large-breasted maenad in four-inch heels. And she was wielding what looked like a ten-inch scimitar. "Come in!" she shrieked. "We've been waiting for you!"

Wendy. Even if I hadn't seen the photograph of her Dania had shown me, I'd have known her by the breasts and the nails and the appallingly puffed-out lips. I tried catching Dania's eye, but Wendy stepped between us. "You!" she said, flourishing the scimitar at me. "You'll tell *me* what you want to say to Dania!"

I glanced toward the window seat. Usually Bess left her mobile on the little table next to it, and, yes, there it was, blinking. "Bess," I said as lightly as I could, "you have a message."

"Oh, Rex," she said vaguely. "A few minutes ago."

Rex?

She smiled triumphantly, reaching back for the phone, but Wendy was too quick for her. She clipped across, amazingly agile in those heels, snatched it up, walked to the French doors, and lobbed it into the spa.

"*What is going on?*" I whispered quickly.

But not quickly enough. Wendy was back between Dania and me. "You think you're so clever, don't you?" she said, baring a set of frighteningly white teeth. "Do you think I am so stupid?"

"I don't think of you at all as a matter of fact," I said coolly. The afternoon with Rex had worked me into a sort of collapse, body and spirit, and all I wanted was a glass of wine and some silence to think back over it. Standing there, I was thinking it over anyway, deciding that, if I wrote it for a Gripp, I'd be able to describe the ease he'd arrived at as a lover of women—not so much in practicing his charms as in delighting in the gift of them, nothing of Pilates in any of it. To be more specific than that would be to risk squeamishness in the reader, particularly for those who, like me, find nothing charming in descriptions of body parts.

"Do you know who I am?" Wendy demanded, stepping right in front of me. "Do you know?"

"I know you've been a damned nuisance," I said. Knife or no knife, this was becoming ridiculous.

"And is this a nuisance, too?" She waved the knife at me. She was breathing hard now, and her breath was foul.

With a lot of luck she'll have a heart attack, I thought, although it was hard to put an age to her with all the work she'd had done. Fiftyish? Sixty? Impossible to tell.

"Ruth," said Bess, "if anyone phones you, please tell them this creature has drowned my phone. I'm going down to my room."

Wendy wheeled around then. "You're not going anywhere!" she shrieked, lunging with the knife.

Had Gladdy not walked in then, back from vespers, Wendy might truly have hooked it into Bess. But, as it was, she wheeled round on Gladdy, who, with the instincts of a fencer, raised her Bible to shield herself, and the knife clattered to the floor. When Wendy stooped to pick it up, Gladdy was too quick for her, stamping down on the flat blade with all her weight.

"You!" screamed Wendy, clawing at Gladdy with the nails.

Bess was the first to land on her, hurling all her considerable weight against her back. And then I ran forward to grab her by the hair. It was slick, like silk, and strands of it were coming off in my hands.

"Aiii!" she screamed. "My extensions!"

"Dania!" I shouted. "For God's sake! Don't just *stand* there!"

She came forward then as if, until I'd suggested it, the thought of doing something about the lunatic she'd brought into our lives hadn't occurred to her. She went to stand over Wendy, speaking to her in the calm, low, purring voice she

used on her regulars. And, as she spoke, Wendy seemed to lose
some of her starch, curling her head and shoulders down like a
caterpillar.

"You stopped taking them again, am I right?" Dania was
saying softly, stroking what was left of her hair.

"Yes," Wendy whispered, eyes on the floor. "Yes, Dania."

I watched in silence, and so did Bess. Even Gladdy, keeping her foot firmly on the knife, seemed intrigued by Dania's
performance.

"Okay," said Dania at last, turning calmly to me. "We will be
going now for a drive, Wendy and me. There is in the car gas?"

☺

à gg, Greece

Put three women together on a Greek island, and sooner or later they
are going to be laughing about sex. Dania, for instance. The other
night, as we all sat out on the veranda under the stars, she came up
with her chicken-and-goat analogy. "On and on until you think, better to
be a goat or a chicken!" she said.

And we laughed, of course, because which of us, especially at our age,
hasn't had such an experience? And which of us, said Bess, didn't take
it personally?

Well, Dania, as it turned out. Not with the chicken-and-goat man ("He
has with intelligent women this problem"), and not with the Sephardic
policeman who liked his women as fat as a house ("He has the soul of
an Arab").

Even Bess laughed at this. What *she* can't stand, she says, are
gymnastics—this position, that position, turn around, stand up, etc.
That's how her last lover was, she says, and you'd think she'd be in
shape after this, but that's not the way it works.

Until I actually met her last lover, I took these tales of gymnastics on faith, putting them together with Bess's theory on fatness and men. But now that I've met him—he arrived the way they all seem to be arriving: without warning—I can't help thinking that if he was a gymnast with Bess, it was surely because he had to be.

But please—please!—before you all write in to tell us how thrilling you find gymnastics or even chicken-and-goat endurance tests, just consider the lilies of the field.

And *kalispera* to all of you.

☙

Ruth, dear, we can't, of course, have any Arab-bashing, and the ending doesn't work at all. Perhaps you're still thinking DGMS? I'm not even going to show this one to Amy until you've fixed it. Also, very snarky about Bess. What's going on there? Could we please return to some local color? Recipes? Pretty please? Sxx

☙

I'm rather confused, Stacey—snark or no snark? First, Amy says she wants something to shake the readers up, and you want recipes? What's going on *there*? Rxx

☙

DINNERTIME CAME AND WENT and still Dania didn't return.

"Think that Wendy murdered her?" Bess said vaguely.

I was worried about just this. What if the woman had a gun in her bag? And had forced Dania onto the ferry? Or worse? "I suppose Dania knows what she's doing," I said.

"Dania?" cried Bess. "That's just the trouble. She's so bloody sure of herself she probably thinks she can talk the devil down from the tree."

"I keep something for Miss Dani?" said Gladdy, looking in from the kitchen.

"Why're you still so dressed up?" said Bess.

Gladdy pressed her lips together. They played this game constantly—Bess demanding answers, Gladdy keeping her secrets. It was becoming tiresome.

"Think I should call Dinny?" Bess said. "Trouble is, the wife is back from wherever she went to."

I shook my head. "What could he do anyway? Scan the whole island? We're just going to have to wait."

"Glad, you go to bed," Bess said. "Ruth and I will wake you if we need you."

When she was gone, we sat in silence—Bess clicking away at her laptop and me in a swoon at last, thinking over the afternoon.

After a while, she looked up. "If it weren't for the voice, I'd say that Wendy was a trannie."

"I know. But she's a she."

"How do you know?"

"She has a son, also psychotic. And she had an affair with Amos."

"*What?*"

Before I could even regret blurting this out, a key turned in the front door and Dania was standing before us, her shoes in her hand.

"*What happened?*" we both asked at once. Her eyes and hair were wild, quite as wild as Wendy's.

I got up and went over to her. "Come and sit down," I said. "Shall I bring you some supper? Where's Wendy?"

She let me lead her to her chair and then sat there, staring straight ahead.

"Miss Dani?" Gladdy called up.

"Go back to bed, Glad!" Bess shouted. "She's home. She's fine."

"Coffee?" I said. Dania drank coffee like water, and had even bought a percolator when we'd first arrived, keeping it going the way she did at home, day and night.

For a while, she just sipped at the mug, saying nothing. But then she looked up and said, "She fell from the cliff. She's gone."

"*What?*" said Bess. "*Which cliff?*"

But Dania just stared down into the empty mug now.

"Where were you?" I asked gently. "Which part of the island?"

"We took back from the restaurant that quick cut," she said.

"Shortcut?" said Bess.

"Over the mountain," she said, "where once we walked."

"*That goat path?*"

She nodded. "There were goats."

"So what happened?" Bess said.

"I would like another cup of coffee, please, Ruthi." And this time she did look up. She looked so long and hard at me that I knew she had more to say, but wouldn't say it until we were alone.

Bess followed me into the kitchen. "There's something fishy going on," she whispered. "Why isn't she calling the police?"

Of course there was something fishy. "Daniushka," I said, bringing her the coffee, "we should call the police. What's Wendy's surname?"

She looked up sharply. "Who wants to know her name?"

"The police will want to know. Someone's going to have to look for her."

"The police?" she said, suddenly alive. "Why the police?"

"Because," said Bess, "Wendy has fallen off a cliff. She may be dead."

"Tompkins," Dania said. "With a *P*."

Bess went to stand in front of her. "Listen," she said, "we should phone the police right now." It was the closest I'd ever seen her come to righteousness. "Or, at least, we should phone Dinny."

But Dania just looked at her watch. "Already it's ten o'clock," she said. "You are going now to phone your taxi driver and make trouble for him?"

"Well, what do you propose?" said Bess.

"Go!" Dania said. "Go ahead! Phone him!"

"Agh," said Bess. "This is impossible. I'm going to bed."

As soon as she was gone, Dania got up and beckoned me to her room. There she closed the door, pulled off her sweater, and held out her naked arms. They were bleeding, scored shoulder to wrist with deep oozing scratches.

"Good God!" I whispered. "What happened?"

"I need for them anti-skeptic," she said. "And look here—here she bit me." She turned her left hand over, and, yes, I could see tooth marks at the base of her thumb.

"All we have is ouzo," I said. "I'll fetch it."

"Ruthi," she said when I returned with the bottle, "I will drink some first. It will help with the shock." She took a long swig, grimacing like a child, then poured it over her arms, wincing as she did. Then she lay back on the pillows, staring up at the ceiling. "It is worse than poison this uzi," she said, slurring the words.

For the first time in her life, she was drunk.

๑

à gg, Greece

There is a track, really a goat path, that we walk on. It is particularly
wonderful when the wildflowers are out, as they are now. But, like so
many wildflowers, these wilt almost immediately when cut. There's a
metaphor to be found in most ephemera, I suppose, particularly for
women of our age. But none of us cares much for such metaphors—I
can't bear lessons from nature; Dania says it's people she's interested
in; and Bess doesn't know what a metaphor is and has no interest in
finding out.

Still, making my way up the goat path, I stop to admire the view.
Poppies, anemones, buttercups, chamomile, daisies, thistles—never
mind my aversion to lessons, I can't help thinking, standing there, that,
at seventy, if I have ten good years left, I will consider myself lucky.
I decide that, from now on, I shall train my mind out of its lassitude
and refuse to throw even an hour of my time away.

When I announce this at dinner one evening, Dania says, For this you
must practice great vigilance. This astonishes me, not because what
she says is so obviously true, but because it had not been obvious to
me before. Practicing vigilance, clearly, is an essential first step. The
next is arming oneself against the disappointment of others. It is this,
perhaps, that I find the most difficult.

But why? Why does the disappointment of another, even another of
little account, have such power to muzzle and chain the free will? This,
says Dania, can be traced back to childhood (a formula she seems to
apply to almost anything, including constipation). Still, I am no longer
a child, and certainly understand the gratification of praise. Is it
gratification, then, that has me handing over my time as if it has no
value? Is it this that had me agreeing to talk to a group of aspiring
writers at the English bookshop next week, unable to disappoint even
the unpleasant owner, who affects such a superiority to detective

fiction? And all because, for once, she'd managed to smile as she asked?

I don't know, I'll probably never know. But I decide that, the next time I walk up the goat path, I'll try to consider the lilies of the field. And take a lesson from them.

◉

AS IT TURNED OUT, WENDY had, indeed, fallen off a cliff. Dania had pushed her. This didn't come out all at once, of course. First I had to hear of the drive around the coastal road to the little tourist restaurant on the other side of the island. "All the way," said Dania, "I talked, she listened like a baby."

"Daniushka," I said, "please tell me exactly what happened." We were on her bed, propped up side by side on pillows.

She sighed. "At first she was calm, eating like a pig, which she is, and drinking, too."

"And then?"

"When we were drinking coffee I told her she must not again come to the house, she was breaking our rules."

"So?"

"So then she starts again screaming, there in the restaurant. Rules? What rules? she shouts. She's going to do this and tell that—crazy things, the usual. So I said, Wendy, you must take your medication—she is, of course, psychotic—but, I should have known it, this question was driving her even more crazy. She starts throwing the dishes, there in the restaurant. So finally I said, Come, Wendy, come. Now we are going."

"And you drove up the goat path?"

She nodded. "I wanted a place totally uninhibited."

"But what about that farmhouse? What about that dog?"

"No dogs, no people where I stopped. Just goats."

"Dania, how on earth did you maneuver the car up there?"

"I am good with such roads."

"In a tank perhaps, not a Fiat."

This she waved off. "There is still uzi?"

I handed her the bottle.

"While we were driving, she was quiet again like a baby because she was frightened we would be rolling over. But when I got to the top, before even I have put on the brake, she's climbing out, running up and down like a mad person, screaming, 'Help! Help!' So, I jumped out, too. Meanwhile, the car is rolling over the edge because I forgot the brake. And she comes to greb me, scretching like a cat, so I greb her—oy, Ruthi," she said. "I don't feel so good. The room is turning. I am going now to throw up."

I helped her to her feet and she staggered to the bathroom, where I heard her retching, gargling, cleaning her teeth.

"Ruthi," she said, coming back into the room, "I learned in the army a few things. So I got her from behind in a grip, nothing she could do, and I gave to her a small push. Now I think I am again going to throw up. Or maybe not."

I closed her door softly behind me, crept along the passage like a thief, and into my room. It was bright with the moon, and the night was warm. I locked the door and then lay on top of the covers, my heart thundering in my chest.

All these years I'd watched with amusement as Dania negotiated the depths and shallows of whatever terrain lay between her and where she wanted to be. Rules, laws, statutes—these were there to be conquered one way or another. And if she happened to fail in the conquest, well, she suffered no fears as to the consequences. "I got this time a jerk," she'd say. "Next time I do it another way."

And now this.

❧

Hester #6

When Saul left Hester for another man, and Lily announced that she wanted to go with him—then, for the first time, I was afraid for the girl. I mean, physically afraid. I'd seen Hester's violence as a child, practiced on other children and, later, on the things she tore and gouged at home—hers, mine, ours. Her rage ran very deep, I knew, while mine flared, strong and quick and searing, and then was gone.

But, until then, Lily had been spared. She had come to understand quite quickly, I thought, the power she held over her mother—the power her words might hold as well, including words she'd not yet spoken. So she said very little, as if she were hiding the words away before they could even be thought.

❧

I SAT AWKWARDLY AT BREAKFAST, thinking I'd wait for Dania to finish her coffee before bringing up the police again.

"Never again I will drink that uzi," she said at last. "How can you stand it, Ruthi?"

"I've grown to like it."

"Look it," she said, trying to rally her old voice. "Today we'll fix everything."

"'We'?"

She narrowed her eyes at me. "Ruthi? What are you saying? Be clear with me."

I looked at the familiar Magyar face—the skin sallower than ever, the eyes bloodshot. "I'm saying as clearly as I can that I will not be an accessory to a homicide. After the fact."

"This is not one of your novels," she said with a sarcastic smile. "After all these years? I can hardly believe it."

"Years or months would make no difference in such a situation, and friendship has nothing to do with it." Perhaps, I thought, she was right about childhood after all. Mine, rife with emotional manipulations, had schooled me against the sort of elementary maneuvers she was trying on me now.

"Do you at least have for me an aspirin?" she said, putting a hand to her head. "Or is that out of the question, too?"

I stood up and went for the aspirin. And when I returned, Gladdy was in the kitchen doorway, holding the scimitar. "Miss Dani," she said, "what I must do with the knife of that lady?"

Dania waved her off dismissively. "Throw it away," she said.

"No!" I said. "You'll need it as proof."

"So now you don't mind being an accessory?" she said, the smile back in place.

"Oh, for God's sake, Dania, this is not a game! And where, by the way, did she get that thing?"

"Amos gave it to her. Cheap junk from the Old City."

"What cheap junk?" said Bess, yawning. She was at least an hour earlier than usual for breakfast. "God! What happened to your arms?"

"Wendy happened," I said. Perhaps, I thought, handing Dania the aspirin—perhaps I could find a way to resuscitate Gripp after all. It would redeem at least a part of this nightmare.

"I'll have some aspirins after you," said Bess. She was looking almost as wan as Dania. "Glad, make me some fresh coffee, please. Strong, very strong."

But Gladdy didn't move. "Miss Ruthi," she said, "I lock up the knife in my room?"

"Good idea," said Bess. "You can't imagine what she's got locked up in that room. Come to think of it, where are my pearls, Glad? The long rope?"

"I got them safe."

"From whom?" I said, bristling a bit. "Or from what?"

"From Rex," said Bess, tossing back her wonderful hair. "He wouldn't be above hocking a rope of pearls. He hocked my diamond and sapphire bangle, and then bought it back at twice the price when Gladdy threatened him with the police."

"*What?*"

"Oh yes!" said Gladdy, quite unusually gleeful. "You must watch out for your things, Miss Ruthi."

I knew Bess was watching me, but I couldn't help it, I flushed. The fact was, Rex had, indeed, fingered the antique tiger's claw I wore on a chain round my neck, and also the chain itself. "Early Raj?" he'd said. "Would you take it off so I can have a closer look?"

"You should read *Chéri*," I said to Bess. "Colette."

"Oh, I *adore* Colette!" said Bess, who had an abiding power to astonish me. "I've read them all. But Rex wasn't playing games, I assure you. He fancies himself in a James Bond film."

The phone rang in my room and I ran to get it.

"Ruth?" said Rex. "Are you at the house?"

"Where else?"

"I've been trying Bess, but there's no answer. Is she all right?"

I stood where I was, examining the towel drying over the balcony chair.

"Ruth?"

"Her phone drowned in the spa."

"Lord! How?"

"A whole new drama."

"I'll be up in a tick." But he didn't hang up. "Listen, Ruth," he said, "yesterday was a marvelous surprise. Thank you."

Surprise? Thank you? I gathered my jewelry from the bedside table and shoved it under my pillow. Then I went to the bathroom to run the water for a shower and a hair wash. Whatever surprises he still had in store—whatever the nature of his devotion to Bess—I wanted to improve on the hag looking back at me from the bathroom mirror before he arrived.

❧

HE WAS THERE WHEN I emerged from my room, chatting quite amiably with Bess.

"He thinks we should get Dinny to take us up the goat path," she said.

Us? I'd never known her to climb anywhere willingly except up to Finn's room or onto the window seat. "We'd have to walk, you know. No one but Dania would dream of taking a car up there. And the car's over the edge, like Wendy."

"Dania's gone up there already," Bess said. "Rex, give me your phone."

There was between them such domestic intimacy, and she was so clearly in charge, that I relaxed, despite myself, into observing them.

"Dinny?" she whispered into the phone. "You alone? You come here? Soon? Quick?" She snapped the phone closed. "Okay, he's coming."

Gladdy came panting in from the outside steps. She was

dressed in her church clothes again, her church bag over her arm. She went to stand before Bess, her back to Rex. "What I must tell them at church?"

"Tell them nothing. Ruth and Rex are going up the mountain to look."

❧

ALL THE WAY UP THE mountain I wondered how Dania could possibly have thought of maneuvering the car there. Tanks or no tanks, she was an appalling driver, talking her way out of traffic tickets the way she talked her way out of everything. Maybe, I thought, she didn't come up here at all this morning, just took the bus down to the port to catch the ferry to Athens and then a plane to somewhere safe.

"There she is," said Rex. He'd been taking care not to touch me, even casually, but now he took my arm and pointed.

And, yes, there she was, sitting on a rock, quite still, the wind whipping around her. I zipped up my jacket. If this was where she'd stopped with Wendy, she was right, it certainly was the perfect spot for a murder. I walked to the edge of the cliff and peered over. The wind had blown the grass and flowers almost flat. The place was bleak, bare, lonely, and I didn't blame Wendy for going wild.

Rex dropped to his hands and knees and crept forward, laying himself flat to look over the edge. "There's the car all right," he said. "Must've done a nosedive. Come and see."

But I was watching a trail of dust make its way up the mountain, a motorbike leading the way. After a while, it came to a halt just down the hill, and Dionysos climbed nimbly off the back.

"*Yasas!*" he said, trying hopelessly to plaster his hair down in the wind.

Dania stood up then, pointing gravely down toward the car, as if she expected him to retrieve it for her.

"Did you tell him that Wendy is down there?" I asked her.

"Why don't you tell him?"

"Down there," I said to him, ignoring the sarcasm. "Crazy woman." I twirled a finger at my head.

"*Ne, ne,*" he said, turning to the young man who'd driven the Vespa. "Yorgos," he said. "Son of Ellie."

I'd seen the boy roaring through town on the bike, with his earring and his aviator glasses and thicket of black curls.

"I will go down there," he said, rolling his trousers up to the knee. "I will do it."

☙

à gg, Greece

We've been having a wonderful time in the kitchen, the three of us. Spring is well along, bringing with it the farmers and their spring produce. They line up along the park wall down at the port, gnarled hands and battered old scales at the ready, offering new cucumbers, peppers, zucchini, eggplant, radishes, lemons. There are even a few early melons and pistachios. It's months too early for the wonderful sweet tomatoes they sell later in the summer, but there is always fresh feta, and also a soft cream cheese, sheep or goat and indescribably delicious. It costs a lot and is worth it. There is also local honey to have with it. Lettuce, endive, and much else can be had in the market.

When we want a change from the moussaka Gladdy's Greek friends showed her how to make, Dania and I take over. You might think you'd never tire of moussaka, but take it from me, an excess of it makes you want to run a mile from anything béchamel. Better to consider an eggplant salad, especially if it's too early for the full-blown dirigible variety.

Here's a recipe we favor:
6 small eggplants cut into cubes
½ cup olive oil
½ cup chopped onion
4 garlic cloves chopped (you might use less if you want to be loved)
½ cup chopped olives (we prefer the wrinkled, strong-tasting ones)
fresh oregano
fresh mint
salt and pepper to taste

Preheat the oven to 425°.

Salt the eggplant and bake in olive oil until soft (about half an hour).

When cool, mix with feta and chopped olives.

Mix ½ cup olive oil, juice of one lemon, onion, garlic, oregano, and mint in a small bowl and pour over eggplant mixture. Toss.

Serve on rounds of French bread or melba toast.

⟳

Ruth, dear, great that you're all back in the kitchen! My assistant, who's something of a foodie, says you left out the feta in the list of ingredients. Would you check to see whether anything else was left out? Also, it would be good to know the name of the wrinkled olives (love 'em, don't you?) and that cream cheese: Is it sheep or goat? And could you give us its name, too? And resend ASAP? We're keen to get it into the food issue, closing Friday. Sxx

⟳

THERE WERE THREE WEEKS TO go before the first of the children would arrive, and Dionysos was supervising the cleaning of his aunt's house down the hill. His wife was in Athens, Bess reported, threatening him with lawyers. She was always threatening him, she said, she'd even threatened to go to the police about Wendy when Yorgos found the heel of a woman's shoe.

Except that it wasn't Wendy's.

"Not high enough for that pig!" said Dania, in high glee herself. It was as if Yorgos, failing to find Wendy's body, absolved her from blame. "It's a miracle!" she crowed. "Like the bread and the fishes."

"Until she hacks back into your e-mail," said Bess from her perch in the window. "Or barges in here with a gun next time."

Dania shrugged. "Let her heck, let her barge, why do I care?"

And she didn't. Even when the goat farmer told his wife he'd heard screams that night, and she told her friends, and the friends told the policeman's wife at church on Sunday, and then Gladdy told them all that, yes, a woman had come screaming into our house with a knife and Dania had taken her away in the car—even then Dania was quite sure the miracle would hold.

She was still sure when the policeman himself turned up at the house with Eleftheria. "Get for me that knife, please, Gladdy," Dania said quite pleasantly. And, with Eleftheria interpreting, she demonstrated for the policeman how the woman had wielded it. "I have for many years," she said, "been for that woman a psychotherapist." And when Eleftheria seemed to have trouble untangling words from word order, she turned to me and said, "Ruthi, please explain to this man."

◠◉

Sorry, Stacey! Greeks are inspired cooks and seem to proceed by instinct. So, I've got into a sort of grab-and-throw habit myself. Like going the wrong way down one-way streets, which I do here all the time. But that's no excuse for leaving out the feta, and much else. See the corrected recipe below.

p.s. that soft cheese is called ξυνομυζήθρα, which translates to something like "ksynomyzithra." It's a more acid version of mizithra, a curdled goat and/or sheep's milk cheese—sometimes more goaty, sometimes more sheepy. Hope that helps. Ruth

Eggplant salad (corrected)
6 small eggplant, cut into cubes
salt and pepper to taste
olive oil for baking
1 cup diced feta
½ cup chopped Kalamata-type olives
Dressing
½ cup olive oil
1 lemon
½ cup chopped onion
4 garlic cloves, peeled and chopped (you might use less if you want
*   to be loved)*
1 tablespoon fresh oregano, finely chopped
1 tablespoon fresh mint, finely chopped

Preheat the oven to 425°.

Salt and pepper the eggplant to taste and bake in olive oil until soft (about half an hour).

When the eggplant is cool, mix in a bowl with the feta and chopped olives.

In another bowl, mix ½ cup olive oil, juice of one lemon, onion, garlic, oregano, and mint until well combined. Pour the dressing over the eggplant mixture. Toss.

Serve on its own or with bread.

⟲

"SO," SAID DANIA, AFTER THE policeman and Eleftheria had left, "that is that."

"Not quite!" said Bess. She was in a fever of discontent now, and it wasn't because of Wendy, I knew; it was Rex. After our excursion up the mountain, he'd asked me back to the hotel for a bite of lunch, as if we'd had it all arranged. If he'd done this to annoy Bess, I didn't much care and, really, there wasn't much revenge in it either. It was just a small reprieve from the drama of Wendy, and also the old charm of lunching with a new lover, the afternoon to look forward to, and a carafe of cool white wine to take the edge off any awkwardness.

"I'm leaving tomorrow," he'd said over coffee. "My yacht's come in. Would you do me a favor and wait till I've gone—say, lunchtime tomorrow—before you tell Bess?"

And so I had waited. And, of course, she'd felt very left out. "God knows how he came up with the money," she grumbled. "You didn't give him any, did you, Ruth?"

I laughed. "That's about as likely as my sailing off in a boat myself."

But then, I couldn't help it, I felt sorry for her again. "Listen," I said, "it was you he was here for, start to finish. Like Finn and me."

She shrugged. "I know, I know. But it doesn't help." She tried to return to her magazine, but then flung it away. "Listen, you two," she said, "can we please decide what we're going to do when that lunatic surfaces again?"

Dania waved a hand. "Maybe she's in Turkey surfacing. Maybe in Timbuktu."

I stared at her, this familiar stranger who had managed to talk the car rental agency not only into waiving her responsibility for the wreck, but also into giving her another car at no additional cost. "Amn't I great?" she'd said. "I got for us an automatic! Even if around the corners it squeals like one of those goats!"

à gg, Greece

Short of plastic surgery, sunglasses do more for an aging face than anything else. Even with plastic surgery, Bess, for instance, seems to lose not only years but also some of her ballast when she launches forth in one of her fabulous pairs. She has a whole shelf of them, and seems to choose among them by mood. Whatever the case, they must never match what she's wearing, she says. Matching is déclassé. When Dania suggests that being excessively concerned with the déclassé might be déclassé itself, Bess just points out that anyone who favors the peasant blouses and skirts of the sixties isn't in a position to pronounce on such matters.

Old age Tourette's is how I've come to think of all this. Without warning, it can jump out. This morning, for instance, when Dania was at it again, boasting about the seven languages she's taught herself, Greek soon to be the eighth, I said, "Yes, and they all sound the same— incomprehensible." I was about to go further—to say how excruciating it is, not only for us, but also for the waiter or the shopkeeper, when she

insists on practicing her elementary Greek—when I saw by the
color in her face that I had gone too far. And that it was too late to
apologize.

It's too late, too, when I face the sour woman who runs the English
bookshop and has not had the grace to thank me for addressing her
aspiring writers. I snatch up the book I've just bought, saying neither
"thank you" nor *"efcharistó"* as I usually do, but, as if to myself,
although quite loud enough for anyone to hear, say, "What a
lousy cow!"

About this, however, I am not sorry. On the contrary, now that it's
popped out, I'm elated. I decide to go down the alley to the overpriced
French shop. I want to see if he has another pair of the gorgeous outré
sunglasses Bess bought there last week. I might even try to find
something for Dania as a peace offering, although I'm not that sorry
there either.

⟜ⓔ

BESS, GLADDY, AND I ALL went down to Dionysos's aunt's house
to give it our approval. It was freshly whitewashed, the doors
and shutters painted in island blue. And each of the three floors
was fronted by a large veranda, facing down toward the Aegean.

"Greek," said Gladdy, bending to inspect a corner, "they
know how to clean."

And, indeed, it was spotless—spare, but spotless.

"Wilfie he's coming?" she asked Bess.

Bess jumped as if she'd been shot. "Oh, God, I hope not!
Have you been phoning him again? Behind my back?"

Gladdy pressed her lips together.

"Because if you have, I'm warning you, I'll leave for another
island."

"What about Aggie?" Gladdy said.

"What about her? She can practice her mindfulness on you. Or her mindlessness. Same thing."

"Hai!" said Gladdy, moving off to examine the kitchen.

"But seriously, Ruth," Bess said. "Why don't we just escape? I mean, I don't know how I'm going to cope with the invasion as it is, and if Wilfred does come, I'm truly lost. Santorini is over and, anyway, Dania's there. But what about somewhere like Hydra? I read about it in that Colossus book."

"What Colossus book?" There she was again, springing surprises. "*The Colossus of Maroussi*?"

"That's it! Rex sent it to me when I told him we were coming here." She settled onto one of the built-in couches. "God, these are uncomfortable!" she said. "But listen, I'm serious, Ruth. How are we going to stand them? Even down here? I mean, it's bad enough already without them, no?"

"It's certainly not heaven."

"And it's going to get worse. What the hell were we thinking?"

I let out a long sigh. "It wasn't so bad in the beginning."

"Before Wilfred came. And Finn and Rex. And now it's going to be Agnes and Hester and, oh, God, those children of Agnes's. Can't we just leave them all to Gladdy?"

I laughed. "You really are divine, Bessie! You have no conscience at all."

"None, none. But listen, Dania's got something up her sleeve, I'm totally sure of it. I bet she doesn't even come back from Santorini."

I hadn't thought of that. But now that I did, I thought Bess could be right. "I have a strong idea that Wendy is dead," I said. "How else could Dania be so unconcerned?" I knew I was committing a final betrayal but over the past few days I'd been feeling the sort of creeping dread of catastrophe I'd described in Gripp after Gripp.

Bess sat forward. "You're right!"

"What's more, I don't think it happened where Dania said it did."

"*E-hê!*"

We both jumped. We hadn't noticed Gladdy standing like a pillar in the doorway.

"They will look all around," she pronounced from there, "and they will find her body. Then we know what we have here on this island, and the children they coming."

"What do you mean 'what we have here on this island'?" I said. But, of course, I did know. She meant we had a murderess and, worse than this, had her in the house. And if she thought it was all my fault, I wouldn't have been surprised at that either.

She lowered herself onto the end of the other couch, something I'd never seen her do before. "Bessie," she said, "you must lock your door now. And Dinny he must get his auntie to put locks here, too."

"Oh, for God's sake!" said Bess. "She's not a psychopath!"

But Gladdy just leaned closer. "That woman she doesn't have a heart for other people."

I looked at her. From the moment she'd arrived—from before that, really, from when Bess first brought up the idea of her coming to Greece—I'd considered Gladdy—if, in fact, I considered her at all—as a sort of straight man in a situation comedy. And now here she was, insisting on a truth about Dania I'd never even considered. And she was right. Dania didn't have a heart for other people. Perhaps none of us did. Perhaps what we felt for other people was what we wanted them to feel for us. And if, indeed, we were like this, Dania was more so.

"Gladdy," I said, "she's my old friend, but you are right."

She paid me no attention. For her, I could see, it was Bess who had all her heart. They were enclosed, the two of them, in a sort of loop of love and friendship that I could only marvel at from outside.

᪥

WE TOOK TWO CARS DOWN to the port to meet them—ours and Dinny's. And then there we stood, Bess, Dionysos, and I, all watching the sea for signs of the ferry.

Gladdy had stayed up at the house to prepare a supper for everyone. For the past few days she'd been in a strangely nervous state, uncharacteristically tentative as she dithered between this or that kind of bread, and did Bess think the children would eat moussaka?

"They'll eat what they're given," Bess said, "and you're not to pay any attention to Agnes and her vegan nonsense either, you hear?"

Agnes had always disapproved of Gladdy, Bess explained. As far as she was concerned, Gladdy had been the "enabler" in the arrangement between them (*"En-aa-bler!"* Bess sang. "Can't you just hear it?"), whereas, if Gladdy had just stayed home with her own child like any normal mother, maybe Bess herself would have had to do likewise ("Fat chance of that!" said Bess).

The fact was, she said, Gladdy was scared of Agnes. She'd never admit it, but it was true. She'd been scared of her as a child, and she was scared of her now. And, really, when you considered what a self-righteous bully Agnes was, no wonder Gladdy was so off-balance when she was around.

"Poor Gladdy," she said now. "Two weeks of it to get through, and then more when we return to California."

"It arrives!" Dionysos announced, trying to tame his hair in the wind.

And, yes, there was the ferry steaming around the bluff toward us. Watching it approach, I couldn't help the flutter of excitement with which I seem to greet all arrivals, even those I've anticipated with dread.

It turned around, backed up in a churn of water, and then came to a stop against the dock as the gangway descended.

Throngs of people began to spill out, dodging cars and trucks and buses. It was always like this—chaotic, dangerous, Greek—and I thought suddenly that I should have warned Hester about the cars and buses, although, of course, she'd only have scoffed with delight.

"There's Hester," said Bess.

And, yes, there she came, near the front of the current. "Whew!" she said, coming to wrap me in a hug. "I was convinced you'd go to the wrong dock if there is such a thing here."

"Wrong dock?" said Bess. She and Hester had never much liked each other and probably never would.

Hester gave her a mocking laugh. "She's always going in the wrong direction," she said. "Haven't you noticed?"

"Where's Agnes?" Bess said.

"Her luggage was right at the back. Here comes Lily with the children now."

Lily. Luggage. Children. The flutter of excitement vanished completely.

"Dinny!" said Bess. "You find my daughter? In there? Tall—" She held up an arm. "No, wait! Here she comes!"

Agnes was struggling toward us under the weight of an enormous backpack. "Hello, Ma," she said, wiping sweat out of her eyes. "Hello, everyone!"

"*Plaits* now?" said Bess. "You look like Minnehaha."

"Oh, Ma!" Agnes flung her long arms around Bess.

"Agh, agh, you're sweaty!"

I watched them with a frisson of envy. If I leveled something like "Minnehaha" at Hester I'd have to prepare for a blast, or at least for the sort of bridling that would leave her curt and rude for days. And yet here were Bess and Agnes, both laughing at the sweatiness as Bess pulled her new linen scarf from her neck and used it to mop them both.

"Let's go!" said Hester. "We've been traveling for days, and I could do with a nice hot bath."

෧

Hester #7

I've been thinking of the time I went to visit her in New York, and she was going to a party and had promised to take me along. "But I'm kaput, darling," I'd said. "You go without me." But, no, she wanted me to go. She was counting on me to go, she said.

What she really wanted, I knew, was to show me off. A Gripp had just made it onto the bestseller list at last, and she herself had lost ten pounds and was looking as good as I'd ever seen her.

Okay, I said, okay. So what do I wear?

No one dresses up here, she said, just go as you are.

Jeans? Sandals?

Fine!

As it happened, I was tanned and happy. The next Gripp was finished ahead of schedule, money would be coming in for the last, and Finn would be there to meet me when I returned. While I waited for her to dress, I phoned him. "Come back to me immediately, you old cow," he growled. "I can't stand it here without you."

Half an hour passed, forty-five minutes, and my mood began to darken.

"Hester!" I called out. "What the hell's going on in there?"

"COMING!" she yelled back, her old pugilistic self.

When finally she emerged, I was in high irritation and she was in a dress I'd never seen. It was tight and short and shiny and black, and she'd painted her eyelids black to match. She wore the gold hoop earrings I'd given her for her birthday, and her hair was fashionably wild. She stopped before me, smiling.

I knew what she expected me to say: "I thought we weren't dressing up?" But instead I said, "Don't lose any more weight. You're not vomiting it up, are you?"

So we arrived at the party in our usual mode—irritated with each other. Like all student parties, it was loud and jammed and boozy, and the girls were all madly dressed up. But Motown was blaring, and when someone pulled me onto the dance floor, I danced wildly, Gripp and Finn and the gypsy earrings I'd just bought fueling my joy. One after the other, young men came to dance with me. I was barefoot, sweating, swirling, panting with happiness. Then I saw Hester. She was in the crowd around the edge of the dance floor, unsmiling. And I thought, She lacks joy herself, that's exactly the problem.

When we met for lunch the next day, she was quick to tell me it

had been a bust of a party. And, by the way, she said, what perfume
were you wearing? Still Opium? Or have you moved on to something
a bit less obvious?

⊚

Ruth, dear, sorry to hear you're unhappy with "old age blurting," but it
really was too late to consult you—it would have been the middle of
the night for you—and there was no way Amy was going to have the
Tourette's people coming down on our heads. Perhaps it will help to
know we've been deluged by comments from old age blurters :) Why
not take a look? Most of them sound just as unregenerate as you.
Sxx 😊

⊚

"UNREGENERATE"? I looked up from my laptop. "Who would
have thought she'd even know the meaning of the word?"

"Who?" said Hester. "What word? You have this way of
landing in the middle of something as if everyone knows what
you're talking about."

I shrugged. "Actually," I said, "I was talking to myself."

It had been going on like this for three days—Hester trudg-
ing up to the house each morning and waiting around there for
me to go with them to the beach, or to the port, or to the port on
the other side of the island.

"I thought you were going to give up that ridiculous column," she said.

"So you did know what I was talking about."

She rolled her eyes to the ceiling. "Can we please just *go*, Mum?"

"Listen," I said. "I rented you a car for this very purpose.
Why don't you take it and I'll meet you later?"

"So Aggie and I came all this way to spend time with each other?" She flicked at something invisible on her jeans. "And what about your granddaughter?"

"I thought perhaps I'd take her one of these afternoons to that friend of Eleftheria—the one with the horses." In fact, the idea had just occurred to me but, now that it had, an afternoon with Lily, horses or no horses, seemed like a holiday compared to a day on the beach with the group.

"And the rest of us? Are we supposed to just sit around and wait for you?"

Bess was still asleep, which was a shame because, when she was with me, Hester adjusted her tone from aggrieved to ironic. Despite their dislike for each other, Hester was always trying to inveigle Bess into an alliance against me, as if in jest. She tried this with all my friends, and often she succeeded. But Bess was not to be inveigled, not even after Finn and Rex. In fact, she became quite uncharacteristically grannyish around Hester. "Hester, my dear," she'd say, "your mother is awfully tired. I think we should call it a day, don't you?"

"And what about the birthday?" Hester said now. "Dania's not going to be there, I gather. Which I think is very weird. Well, that's your business, not mine."

"Indeed."

She looked up sharply.

But Bess was coming up the stairs just then. "Hello!" she said, yawning. "You're here bright and early, Hester!"

"How are we going to bear it?" she'd said to me the night before. She'd poured us each a glass of the Cognac Agnes had brought from duty-free, and we'd collapsed onto opposite sides of the window seat. "I knew it was going to be tedious," she'd said, "but already it feels like a life sentence."

"Lily's taken the children to the beach by bus," Hester said to her. "I thought we'd all go and meet them there."

"Not me," said Bess. "I'm still chewing sand from the last beach experience. Glad!" she called out. "How's my coffee?"

"Oh, I'd love a cup of coffee, if I may," Hester said.

"Of course!" cried Bess. "Glad! Make that two cups, please!"

Gladdy came to the kitchen door then, her hands on her hips. "I am make coffee for Miss Bess!" she announced.

"Well, just make some more then," said Bess. "And bring another cup right now, please!"

I saw the color high in Hester's cheeks, and felt rage rising in my own. Gladdy had been peculiar since they'd all arrived, but this was more than peculiar—it was revolution.

"It's like having a bloody lover," Bess said. "She used to try this on with Agnes, too, you know. You just have to stamp it out."

"Oh, hell!" cried Hester, pulling her phone from a pocket. "I meant to text Aggie."

"What's she doing down there?" said Bess. "Her morning devotions?"

Hester laughed. And when Gladdy came in with a cup, she sat back with her coffee as if there were nothing she'd rather be doing than chatting with her mother and her mother's new-found half sister, all of them laughing at "old age blurters," and agreeing that her mother was, indeed, unregenerate, a word Bess did not happen to know, although now that she did know it, she was going to claim it for herself, she said.

❧

à gg, Greece

With children present in our lives, I find myself suffering nostalgia for a time when adults weren't called upon to applaud them for accomplishing life's most minor tricks and tasks. Underwater swimming, for instance. Last night, Bess's daughter silenced the entire table by tapping a knife on a glass and announcing that her nine-year-old had that day learned to swim underwater.

I glanced down to Bess's end of the table, where she was rolling her eyes. She's been rolling her eyes a lot since they arrived, particularly when it comes to this granddaughter, an awkward girl, who, whenever she can, entwines herself around her mother, staring defiantly out at Bess.

Watching the performance, I long to say that, eight or nine years down the line, the girl is going to find out how little the world cares for her swimming underwater or for anything else, and how ill-equipped she'll find herself to make her way without the false encouragement she's come to count upon.

"Dysfunctional," Hester whispers to me.

And I remind myself to tell her how stupid I consider the concept.

But not now. Now we are watching together as the underwater swimmer slips off her mother's lap and returns to her place at the table for pudding. When she arrives, she finds that her younger brother has scooped the topknot of whipped cream from her crème caramel and, whining loudly, she rounds the table again for another session on her mother's lap. At which point Bess pushes her chair back, picks up her crème caramel, and goes to enjoy it in the relative peace of the window seat.

◎

"LISTEN," BESS WHISPERED TO ME. "I spoke to Dinny. Hydra's out of the question—it would take two days to get there. I also spoke to the agent at the port. She said, What about Naxos? Naxos is easy. We could slip away tomorrow."

"And the party?" It was to take place in three days, in the square, and Gladdy had invited the whole village. When we'd objected to this, she'd simply said that she wasn't going to be shamed in front of her new friends, and when Bess still balked, she called in Dionysos for help. "*Ne*," said he, smiling. "Greek party for everyone, *ne*, *ne*!"

"I don't give a damn about the party!" Bess said now. "Who asked for it? Who's paying for it? We are! You and me!"

But I was getting a bit sick of playing the voice of reason. "Okay," I said, "so let's escape."

She eyed me suspiciously. "You mean it?"

I shook my head. "Not really. I'd be worrying too much about shaming Gladdy and wounding Hester. But you could go on your own, why not?"

She pulled a face, picked up her magazine, riffled through it petulantly, then threw it to the floor. "It wouldn't be any fun on my own."

We hadn't heard from Dania, and even though there was some relief in having her gone, it was as if we were now part of the pestilence she'd brought to the island. I saw it in the looks I was getting when I went off for my afternoon walk—the man in the jewelry shop, the restaurant owner, the baker and his helper. Gladdy said that her friends were asking, too. Where had Dania gone? they wanted to know. And *why* had she gone?

"It would make us seem complicit if we left now," I said.

"Complicit?"

"As if we, too, were running away from a murder."

"But we *would* be running away!" cried Bess. "What's wrong with that?"

"Want to do me a favor and write the next column?"

She scowled, she sulked. "You're just changing the subject."

"Why not write about running away from running away?"

"That cow in New York would only ruin the fun."

"I'll deal with her. And it's only three hundred words."

"*Only!*"

I laughed. The children had gone off for a windsurfing lesson and we had the afternoon to ourselves.

"That's how I met Rex, you know," she said. "Windsurfing."

"*Windsurfing?*"

"In the Bahamas. He was the instructor."

"*You* were learning to windsurf?"

"God, no, of course not. I was there with Victor. *He* was learning."

"Who's Victor?"

She tossed back her hair. "I was with them both for a while," she said. "It was lovely."

"They knew about each other?"

"Naturally! We were a sort of trio. Wilfred pronounced them both gay, of course. But then he thinks everything's gay— the table, the chairs, the washing machine, and so forth."

I laughed, I kicked off my shoes. The idea of Rex as a windsurfing instructor had shaken me back into my skin. "So, what happened to Victor?" I said.

"He went back to Paris after a while, or Liège, I think Liège. Said he couldn't stand another minute of English weather. But I think there was a mistress there, or a wife. Or both. So that left just Rex and me."

❦

AND THEN, A FEW DAYS before the party, Rex himself sauntered in. He was very tanned, very blue-eyed. "I've been phoning Bess," he said, "but she's not answering. Any chance of a coffee?"

I glanced into the kitchen. Gladdy and two of her friends were clattering around in there, clucking and gesticulating in what had clearly become a sort of common language among them.

"On second thought," he said, following my glance, "I'll have some later."

I smiled, quite unable now to see him as anything but an aging windsurfer who'd lost Bess her fortune on lampshades. If ever I revived the Gripp series, I thought, I'd bring that in, it would be easy. And I'd talk about the sort of aging woman who'd fall for his sort of charm. And how quickly she'd recover.

Gladdy came to the kitchen doorway, the friends behind her. "Too early for Miss Bess," she said. "Come back later, Mr. Rex."

"You're staying at the hotel?" I asked.

"Well, that's the thing. They're full. A wedding. You couldn't find it in your heart to put me up here, could you?"

I looked away before I found it anywhere in myself to offer him Dania's room. Or mine. Or even the couch.

"You can stay at the hostel, same like Mr. Finn," said Gladdy.

"Mr. Finn? Who's Mr. Finn?"

Gladdy clicked her tongue and turned back into the kitchen.

"What's got into her?" he whispered.

I got up and went through to the kitchen. "Gladdy?" I said.

But she just went on cracking and separating eggs with the other women.

"Listen, Gladdy," I said, "Bess and I don't even *want* this party—"

She whipped around then, her whole face puffed out like a sea urchin. "*I* make the party!" she shouted. "*I* pay for the party, too!" She dug furiously into the pocket of her apron and pulled out her old zipped purse. "See?" She thrust it at me. "See?"

The only time I'd ever seen Gladdy lose her temper like this was on the phone with her grandson. "But, Gladdy," I said, "you shouldn't be paying for any of this."

"Then *who* is paying? *Who?*"

The Greek women stood behind her, two dark, squat pillars in aprons. Clearly she was showing off for them.

But I'd had enough. "*We* are paying for it," I said, "as you very well know. What's happened to the money in the coffeepot?"

"That is not party money!" she spat out. "That is house money!"

House money? Party money? The woman had gone mad. "Gladdy," I said, "how much have you spent? I'll make sure you're paid back."

But she just clicked her tongue and turned on the electric mixer.

"Listen," I said to Rex, coming back into the living room, "you'd better go down to the café for a coffee. And pop into the hostel on the way."

❧

à gg, Greece

Bess here again. I have to say I'm getting a bit sick of the women who write in, wanting us to give them more of a *Shirley Valentine* or *Enchanted April* sort of year. Listen, women, why don't you try it yourselves? Try putting up with the sour looks you get in the morning because you happen to have sampled the honey cake Ruth thought she'd hidden on the top shelf, behind the sugar. I found it, of course—you can't hide food from an addict—and sampled it, and it was so bloody marvelous that, sample by sample, I managed to finish the whole thing.

I mean, can you imagine hiding food? It's like being stuck in one of those English boarding schools with starvation rations and midnight feasts.

And another thing—try having meal after meal with women who keep saying, "No more for me, thanks." Pudding? "No more for me, thanks!" And the preserved oranges I keep buying at the bakery because Ruth loves them? "No more for me, thanks." Meanwhile, I see her pulling in her stomach when she looks at herself in the mirror. The trouble is, she can't pull in the bags under her eyes or lift the sagging jowls—that she can't do, although, of course, she's miles above plastic surgery, that's for women like me—frivolous women who think of nothing but food and clothes and men.

I haven't even mentioned Dania here because Ruth says that that could jeopardize us all. So I'll just say that the closest I've come to the Valentine experience is with my Greek poet. (Ruth says his poetry stinks. She's a snob, of course, and cares more for poetry than for men. Except mine. But that's another story.)

Anyway, back to my poet. Going out to dinner with him is pure pleasure—dishes upon dishes and, of course, puddings. Even yogurt and honey is better than "No more for me, thanks." (The only snag is his wife, who's a cow, and even fatter than I am.)

So, listen, women: If you're going to bolt, don't bolt with other women. And *please* don't write in to say how much you "cherish" an evening or a weekend with your "girlfriends." This isn't an evening or a weekend, it's a whole damned year, and these women are definitely not girls. Take it from me: If you want to get away from husbands and children, get away with a man. *That's* romantic. And it's much more fun.

◎

BESS KNEW, OF COURSE, I'D be reading the piece before sending it off. I had to transcribe everything she wrote because she couldn't type, she could only peck at the keyboard with one finger. And so, typing along, I was stopped suddenly, as if slapped. Bags and jowls? I went to stare into the mirror, and, yes, there they were. And it wasn't even as if I didn't know them intimately—rue them, abhor them. I did, I did. It was just that the wreck that faced me every morning had always seemed, somehow, between me and me, at least until I'd put on makeup and sunglasses. But now, seeing myself as if by mistake through the eyes of a "Granny à Go Go" reader—well, yes, indeed, surgery could only have helped. Even Dania had known this.

I finished the typing and sent the piece off with a breezy note to Stacey. And when I came back into the living room and Bess looked up, expecting God knows what, I said as lightly as I could, "Two days to the party, four till they leave. Have you ever known time to crawl so slowly?"

She didn't answer, just muttered, "I'm sorry, Ruth, chuck it in the bin. I can be a hell of a bitch when I'm jealous."

"Agh," I said, waving this off. "I'm sorry we didn't run away as you suggested. Never mind the party. Never mind Hester either."

She tossed her hair. "They're both bullies," she said, "she and Agnes. And it'll be a battle to the death. Our death. Wherever we are."

So it was over and would remain over, I thought. And if Rex had used me to have her back—which I didn't think he had—well, if he had, I didn't want him back, regardless. It was she, as it turned out, who'd told him to come for the party. She'd told everyone to come, everyone except Wilfred. And just as I was thinking that at least he wouldn't be there, at least that, Agnes and Hester burst in, the children close behind them, and there they stood, like a choir about to sing.

"You're not going to like this!" Hester announced breathlessly.

Agnes let out one of her rare whinnying laughs. "Wilfie is on the one o'clock ferry!" she said.

"And they're bringing the new baby!" said Lily.

"*What?*" Bess sat up, sending her magazine flying.

"And the au pair," said Agnes, "because she's still breast-feeding."

❧

IN THE SILENCE THEY LEFT behind them, Bess took long, deep breaths.

"Listen," I said, "we can show up at the party, stay for a bit, and leave again. What's wrong with that?"

She just shook her head, still breathing loudly.

"Bess," I said, "what's the situation with money?" It was a question I'd been saving for the right moment, and although this wasn't it, I wanted to know what power Wilfred might still be holding over her. "Your grandmother's money?" I said. "It's safe?"

"Sort of. I promised to give some to Rex—"

"Oh, for God's sake, Bess!"

"But I won't," she said quickly. "Don't worry, I won't."

I threw up my hands, as exasperated as if it were my money she were throwing away.

"It sort of keeps him at my side," she said, "like a puppy."

"That says a hell of a lot about his devotion, doesn't it?"

She laughed. "He's devoted to himself. They all are."

"I could almost wish Finn were coming," I said, "just to give Rex a run for your money."

She gave me a sideways glance. "Finn is coming," she said. "But it's supposed to be a secret."

⊚

Hester #8

I laughed when Hugh called his sons bloody aliens. And yet that's just what he'd have in Hester, too—another bloody alien.

The other day, she announced with pride that she was reading through Trollope ("reading through"!). Does she notice, I wonder, how casually Trollope describes the bonds within a family? One child adored, another overlooked, no "shoulds" in the matter? Hester herself is full of "shoulds." Just yesterday she said to me, "Lily's been reading your books, you know. You should ask her what she thinks."

"As if!" as she would say. My suspicion is that when she reads the books, she's on a treasure hunt for signs of herself. Finding none, she pays me back by saying nothing. And, of course, I never ask.

And do I care? In fact, I do. I want us to be able to walk off the narrow stage on which we seem to have confined our drama. I want to be irrationally, unquestioningly, and absolutely in love with her. But, for all this, she remains a stranger—a stranger whose happiness is, somehow, central to my peace of mind, just as mine is a threat to hers.

⊚

"WHAT DOES SHE MEAN, 'downhill sentence'?" demanded Bess. We were on the veranda with glasses of ouzo, enjoying the few hours left before the party was to begin. "I don't see what's downhill about 'the only snag is his wife, who's a cow, and even fatter than I am.' What's she talking about?"

"I think she's saying if you leave it at 'the only snag is his wife,' it'll be stronger. Readers like to work a bit."

"But she *is* a cow, and she *is* fatter than I am!"

"I know, I know. She's also bleached and a termagant. But it might be funnier if you just left it at 'the only snag is his wife.'"

"What's funny about that?" she demanded.

"It's hard to explain funny."

"Anyway," she said, "it isn't meant to be funny."

"That makes it even funnier."

"And I left out 'bleached' on purpose," she insisted, "because they're all bleached here, or dyed dead black, so what's the point? Do you know how long it took me to find someone here who could get my color right?"

I gazed down at the Aegean, brilliant in the afternoon light. The ouzo, which usually lifted my spirits, was only making me maudlin. "*Ille terrarum mihi praeter omnes angulus ridet,*" I murmured.

"Ruth? Are you listening?"

"'This corner of the earth smiles on me more than any other.'"

"But will you tell her not to change it? I don't give a damn about the readers. And what's a termagant?"

How much better it would have been, I thought, to have had Greece to myself. No Bess, no Dania, no Gladdy, no children, and no Wendy.

"And when it's printed in the magazine, I want to make sure she sees it."

"Who?"

"The bleached cow! What's the matter with you?"

I shook myself to attention. "We'll probably be gone by the time a copy reaches here."

"Good! I can't *wait* to be gone! Even Gladdy's getting on my nerves these days. Maybe I'll just fly off and leave her with her church friends and their tiropitas."

I looked at my watch. "Are you ready? It's time to go to the party."

She hauled herself up. "Half a sec, I've got to change my shoes. Those cobblestones are lethal."

⌁

"OH, GOD," SHE SAID AS we came down the slope. "Wilfred and his gang are there already."

I looked down into the crowd, and, yes, there they were— Wilfred and Tarquin and a pale young girl cradling a baby. They were sitting along the far wall, with Lily crouching at their feet, trying to coax Mohammed away from a feral cat.

"Lily!" I said, pushing through to her. "The cats are full of disease. Don't touch them."

But when she scooped Mohammed up, he turned in his rage and bit her hard on the shoulder. "OW!" she yelled.

"He didn't mean it," said Tarquin, taking over the shrieking child.

Lily's eyes were swimming with tears now. "Ow," she said again softly.

"What you do with a biter is to bite him back," I said, examining her shoulder. "You'll have a bruise, but at least the skin isn't broken."

"JESUS CHRIST!" cried Tarquin, pushing the child off his lap. "Wilfred! The little bastard has drawn blood this time! Just look!"

Wilfred gave a dramatic sigh.

"Come, Liliput," I said, taking her by the hand. "Sometimes one is lucky enough to see providence at work."

She looked at me and, for the first time, I saw how astonishingly like Hugh she was—the hair, the jaw, even the tilt of her head as she broke into a smile.

I sat down at an empty table. "What about some wine?" I said. Carafes of red and white had been placed on every table. Gladdy had thought of everything.

"Mum would have a fit," she whispered.

"At *sixteen*? Then we won't let her see, will we? Where is she anyway?"

"Over there, welcoming people. With Agnes."

I turned to look. There they were at the lower entrance, both of them in Greek-style long dresses, like a pair of caryatids.

"It's not nearly as bad as being bitten by a horse, you know," Lily said, examining her shoulder.

With the color high in her cheeks, she really was quite beautiful in an artless, girlish sort of way.

"You're very like your grandfather, you know," I said.

She looked up, startled. "Really?"

"Absurdly so." I filled our glasses with white wine. "And I think he'd very much approve of you."

The plaza was overflowing now, and townspeople kept coming in, their children with them. A lamb was turning on the spit, smoking the air gloriously.

"Ha! There you are!" said Bess. "Seen Rex?"

"It's hard to see anyone except Agnes and Hester. Do you see where they've stationed themselves? There, at the entrance."

She turned. "Oh, God!" she said. "Are they mad? They've gone all empire and ruched."

"Mum bought it specially," murmured Lily, her whole face on fire now.

But it was impossible to stop Bess once her sense of style had been offended. "And bottle green!" she went on. "And that girl glued to Agnes's hip as usual. Oh, God." She looked around disconsolately. "Where is Rex?"

"There he is," said Lily.

Bess stood up. "Oh, there!" She waved to him with both arms. "Rex!" she shouted. "We're over here!"

But, if he heard, he ignored her, pushing on past a table of priests toward where Wilfred and Tarquin were sitting at the far side.

"Ruth!" said Bess urgently. "Would you go over there and save him? Tell him we're here?"

I got up and made my way among the tables, nodding, smiling, thanking, and all the while chasing down the source of whatever it was that was so unsettling me. Rex? It certainly wasn't Rex. Nor was it Bess. Nor even Finn, who was about to turn up out of the blue again. No. It was Hester in that bottle-green dress—all the hope that had gone into it—and Lily like Boudicca, defending her.

The trio along the wall didn't seem to notice Rex approach. But when he took hold of a spare chair from a nearby table and seated himself before the young girl, Wilfred looked up and said, "Relax. I had the DNA done. You're not the father."

Rex ignored him. "Irina," he said, "when are you going home?"

She couldn't have been much older than Lily, and yet she looked ancient, used up—sunless, vapid, pale as water. It was ridiculous to think of her replacing someone as vivid as Bess.

"Irina's staying on in London for a bit," Wilfred said casually. "We're trying for a residency permit for her."

Rex rested his elbows on his knees, knitting his fingers together. "I'd like to see the results of that test, if I may," he said.

"Certainly, certainly. Oh, hello, Ruth. Happy birthday to you."

"Rex," I said, touching his shoulder, "would you like to join us? We're sitting over there."

He glanced up with such a look of sorrow on his face that I thought, He's in love with this sad excuse for womanhood. Or with the idea of her. Or with himself as the father of her child. "I'll be with you in a minute," he said vaguely, turning back to the girl.

☙

à gg, Greece

One of the best things about our joint birthday party was that we didn't have to do a thing to prepare for it—or, better still, clean up afterward. Gladdy ran the show with the help of her friends in the village. For her, and for all of us in different ways, this was the real culmination of our year.

The women had been preparing for days—our kitchen, their kitchens. And then, on the night before the party, their husbands trussed the lamb, dressed it, set up the rotisserie, and loaded the wood. In this way, on the day itself, the lamb was turning on the spit before the first guests even arrived.

(The recipe below is provided simply to give you an idea of what's involved in preparing lamb on the spit. It does not begin to approach the complexities of choosing, dressing, trussing, and basting a thirty-pound lamb. If you are determined to try this for yourself, I'd suggest a trip to Greece in the late spring, and an apprenticeship of several weeks or even months to a willing mentor.)

Basting sauce for lamb on the spit
best quality olive oil
5 or 6 cloves garlic, peeled and crushed
fresh Greek oregano, rosemary, and sage
lemon juice
salt and pepper

There should be 4 or 5 cups of basting sauce for a 30-pound lamb, and it should be basted inside and out with a bundle of fresh oregano, rosemary, and sage sprigs throughout the roasting. The cooking will take 4 to 5 hours.

❧

I'D WRITTEN THE OPENING OF the column days before the party, thinking that, failing all else, I'd fill in with recipes afterward. There were still three columns left to do before the year was up. Bess would certainly be on strike after the downhill-sentence standoff, and there was no point in even considering Dania. I was just starting to say something about this to Bess—anything to lure her away from the sight of Rex and the au pair—when, suddenly, down the steps in a swirl of musk came Dania herself, arms wide like a conquering heroine.

"*Daniushka!*" I cried, jumping up.

"What?" said Bess, turning around at last.

"*Ruthi!*" Dania threw her arms around me. There were tears in her eyes, real tears. "I was without you like an orphant!"

"Here," said Dionysos, standing to give her his chair. "Sit down, please, here. You want lamb? You want fish?"

She took my hand in hers and held it tight. "You can't imagine how exhausted I am!" she said. "Every day Yael is sailing in the water with the children, and every day I am cleaning and cooking, can you imagine?"

"Miss Dani?" Dionysos was almost bowing to her now. "You want lamb? You want fish?"

She looked up vaguely. "Lamb," she said, "but not bloody, please."

I glanced at Lily, who was gazing at her in amazement.

"Always," Dania went on, returning to her lament, "always she was keeping me under her eyes. If I took for myself extra time with the patients, she went off the handle. Can you imagine this?"

I looked at her in wonderment. She was back as if she'd left nothing behind.

"We've had children here, too," said Bess grumpily, pouring herself more red wine. She'd had several glasses already, and would soon, I knew, become belligerent. "*And* their children. *Including* the one that they're adopting. *And* its mother. *And*, as it happens, its father as well."

Dania cocked her head at me.

"Except that Rex is *not* the father," I said. I'd given her this news several times already, but clearly it didn't help.

She huffed around in her chair. The party was showing no signs of winding down, and clouds of mosquitoes were beginning to sing around us.

Dionysos arrived with Dania's plate. He placed it in front of her like a waiter, one hand behind his back.

And behind his back, too, I saw his wife approaching.

"Oh, for God's sake!" muttered Bess. "This is all we need."

But she was smiling this time—not at me, apparently, or at anyone, but still she was smiling.

"If she spits on me again," whispered Bess, "I'll kill her. I'm telling you, I will."

Despite the weather, the woman was wearing some sort of fake fur collar over a gold brocade jacket. Bright gold earrings hung from pendulous earlobes, and her feet were squashed into gold shoes.

Dania smiled up at her. "*Parakalo!*" she said. "*Parakalo!*"

"It's '*kalispera*,'" I murmured.

"Dania!" said Bess. "Could you *please* get a move on so they can serve the cake?" She turned to Dionysos for help, but he was standing behind his wife now, the ideal courtier—sober, proud, silent.

Dania looked down at the plate in front of her. She stabbed at the meat. "Is it lamb or is it goat?" she said. "Goat I don't like."

"Just *eat* it!" cried Bess in exasperation. And Lily let out a small squeal of fright.

"No goat!" Dionysos said, stepping forward.

"No goat!" said his wife definitively.

I stood up quickly and put a hand on Lily's shoulder. "This is my granddaughter," I said to the wife. "*Engoní.*" I'd had the word at the ready for just such a circumstance. "From California."

"*Yasas, yasas,*" she said, baring an uneven set of cigarette teeth in a smile.

"Maybe I fetch for myself the lamb," said Dania. "Whatever he says, this smells like goat."

But this was too much for Bess. She leaned across the table to Dania. "*For God's sake!*" she hissed. "Finish your fucking goat! Can't you see everyone's waiting for you? Or don't you care?" She slapped at her elbow. "What's the bet these mosquitoes don't even bite Greeks?" she said.

"Gott!" Dania muttered, putting her knife and fork together and pushing the plate away. "I ate already on the ferry a sandwich."

And then, as if on cue, Gladdy beckoned us to the cake table. She'd given up trying to light the candles, she said—the wind kept blowing them out. So, we stood on either side of her like schoolgirls while the crowd broke into loud song.

à gg, Greece (conclusion)

Birthday cake, or Ruth's grandmother's Victoria sponge
(For two 8-inch layers)
butter to the weight of 4 eggs
sugar to the weight of 4 eggs
flour to the weight of 4 eggs
4 eggs
a bit less than 6 tablespoons whole milk, warmed but not hot or it will curdle the eggs
1 teaspoon vanilla essence
1 ½ teaspoons baking powder

With an electric mixer, beat butter and sugar until creamy.

Add flour and eggs, alternating.

Add a little milk as needed to make the mixture smooth.

Add remaining flour and eggs.

Add vanilla essence.

Add baking powder.

Pour into two 8-inch buttered and floured baking tins.

Bake at 350° for 25 to 30 minutes.

೨

THE LIGHTS WERE BLAZING IN the house when we got back. Somehow, Gladdy had got there before us and was sitting on the couch again, this time with the policeman.

"What's going on, Glad?" said Bess.

Gladdy clicked her tongue. "He come for Miss Dani," she said.

The policeman stood up soberly, nodding to Dania.

"Is there even a jail on the island?" Bess whispered. The drama with Dania seemed to have sobered her completely.

"What is the problem?" said Dania.

But the policeman just shrugged. He pointed to the door.

"I must go with you?" she said, walking her fingers to illustrate. Presumably, she didn't have any Greek for the question.

He nodded.

"Ruthi," she said, "please keep with you your phone. I will soon be back."

"Listen," said Bess after they had left, "that woman can talk her way out of anything."

"*E-hê!*" said Gladdy. Perhaps even she had had some wine, I thought.

I looked at my watch. Midnight. In two days Hester and Agnes would be leaving. Two months ago, a ferry had gone down between one island and another, only the crew surviving. And just as I was wondering how to suggest to Hester that she find a seat for them near the lifeboats without her exploding into the mocking laugh, she burst in in a flurry of bottle green.

"Have you seen Lily?" she shouted. "Where did she go?"

Her face was scarlet, her hair wild. "She's with that thug again!" she said, looking round. "I just know she is!"

"Thug?" said Bess. "What thug?"

"Eleftheria's son!" shouted Hester. "That car mechanic!"

"Don't be such a snob!" said Bess. "He's drop-dead gorgeous! Wow! Lily!"

"Yes," I said, joining in. "Wow!"

"You're both ridiculous!" said Hester. "I'm going to find Eleftheria." And she raced out again.

Gladdy sat up. "They going to lock up Miss Dani for good?" she said happily. Certainly she must have had some wine.

I walked onto the veranda. For better or for worse, I thought, Dania will be fine. All these years I'd seen her talking her way around immigration officials, flight attendants, traffic police, university administrators. "Amn't I great, Ruthi?" she'd say. "I give myself a raving review!"

"I don't know what I want, you know," said Bess, coming to stand next to me.

"*Nil desperandum.* Rex will tire of her."

"But I don't even want him back. I want something without words for it. Like Lily. Tonight."

"Something new? Something to look forward to?"

"Those are just words," she said impatiently. "Anyway, I'm not asking for an answer, I'm just telling you I want something without a word for it. I always have. Only now I know I'll never find out what it is."

"Oh, Bessie," I said, reaching out for her hand. The night was soft and the moon full. It was the way it had been when we'd first arrived.

"Maybe that's the thing about old age," she said. "We understand that we can never know."

I saw a tear meandering down her cheek.

"And we can't do anything about it either," she said. "I mean, we're stuck with ourselves, this one life."

"*Timor mortis conturbat me.*"

"You're always doing that!" she said. "Showing off!"

"'Fear of death disturbs me.'"

"Oh."

❧

THERE WAS NO GOING TO bed that night, at least not for me, because, just as we were coming in from the veranda, Eleftheria burst in, still dressed in her party finery, with Hester close behind her.

"What's happened?" I said.

"Yorgos he is a good boy!" Eleftheria cried. "Good boy!"

"Yes," I said, "we know that. What's the matter? What's going on?"

She grabbed my hand and kissed it.

"He's gone off with her!" Hester shouted. "That's what's the matter!"

"With *Lily*?" I said, my heart leaping to my throat. "Where with Lily?"

"To *beach*!" Eleftheria said desperately. "Boys and girls. I tell her!"

"*Which* beach?" said Hester. "*Where* is this beach?"

I put my hand on Eleftheria's shoulder. "How did they get there?" I said slowly. "Car? Bus? How?"

"Oh!" She laughed. "Motorbike!"

"*See?*" Hester cried.

I certainly could see. I saw him roaring Lily down the mountain, leaning this way and that way through all the twists and turns, and if they flipped over the edge, like Wendy, they'd be just another break in the fence.

"Come," I said, grabbing the keys and leading the way to the car. "Eleftheria, you sit in front to show me the way."

We raced down the hill, Hester silent for a change. Go here, Eleftheria said, go there. And then, at last, "There! There!"

I swerved onto a grassy outcropping and stopped behind a flock of Vespas.

"I show you," said Eleftheria, taking off her shoes.

We could hear them as we climbed down the hill—laughing, shouting, singing—and I stopped for a moment. The sound of their voices in the moonlight, the swish and salt of the sea, had filled me suddenly with the sort of happiness I'd forgotten over all these years—the happiness that comes with a night on a beach with a boy, with the laughing and singing and a whole life left to live.

◎

DANIA WAS BACK WHEN WE returned, flopped into a chair, with the policeman standing behind her. "Gott!" she said. "Am I tired!"

"Daniushka! *Already*? What happened?"

"Come, come!" she said to the policeman. "You want a cup of coffee? A glass of uzi?"

"*Parakalo!*"

"Ruthi? Would you fetch for him a glass of uzi?"

There was nothing for it but to play her slave, certainly with the policeman settled in place now next to her.

"They found Wendy, can you believe it?" Dania said. "I had to identify the body." She shook her head in a perfect show of grief. "Terrible," she said, "and terrible smell!"

"Where?" said Bess.

I shivered. Amos, Wendy, and who next?

The policeman emptied his glass and stood up, smiling around awkwardly. "*Efcharistó!*" he said. "*Efcharistó!*"

"Where did you see the body?" I asked as soon as he was gone.

Dania sighed. "Down there at the hospital. They had it in the morgyoo."

A snort from Bess. "And they didn't wonder how she died?" she said.

"They wondered," Dania said. "I told them she was violent, she was screaming. The woman was crazy, what can I say? So, let's now all go to bed. It's already morning."

☙

à gg, Greece

Now that we're nearing the end of our year, I begin to count up all the things we've been free of here, and don't really want to go back to. Clearly, children aren't one of them as they've been with us, one way or another, from the start. But what we don't have is anyone wishing us a good rest of the day—at least not that we know of. Ditto, no one has been reaching out. And sharing is reserved for goods divided up. Telling someone the news is not sharing it; it's telling someone the news. On the other hand, if you offer a drinker a glass of your wine, you are sharing, however inadvisably, not enabling. If your offer is refused, you'll get a "no thanks," not an "I'm good," which answers a question that hasn't been asked. Here we have problems, certainly, but not issues. Vegetables are not veggies. And at a restaurant, you won't be asked if you're enjoying your meal, certainly not whether you're still working on it. Fortunately, we enjoy good health, no thanks to the wellness bulletins that come in regularly from our health insurers. "Let's not go there" means, literally, "Let's stay where we are or go somewhere else." Parenting doesn't happen here; neither does birthing. And when people die, they die. When they pass, they do so in a car or on foot and, after they've passed, they're still here, on earth [*sic*], which may also be a planet, but so what? Hopefully means full of hope (although I'm almost ready to give up on this one). And when you're "on the same page," you're reading the paper together. The halt, the crippled, the feeble minded, etc., may be challenged or differently abled, but they are also unfortunate. And when you sign off on something, you actually put your signature on a contract. For someone over the age of about nine or ten, things might be frightening, but they are not scary. They might be delicious, even fabulous, but they're not yummy. I've already dealt with the plague of "love you," so we can pass over that and onto a few of the words and phrases, once so alive in the black community, that suffer instant death when uttered by middle-class whites: "sistah," "girlfriend," even, God help us, "cool"— we've had none of this here. No one hitting the ground running either, not even at the end of the day or 24/7 BTW. And no one except tourists trying to be mindful. What we do love is the canopy of stars that show up every night. They make us want neither to lean in nor to reach out. We just sit out on our veranda with our glasses of ouzo and can of DEET, and if anyone says, "OMG, how cool is this?" we'll give them a dose of it.

☙

I MIGHT HAVE KNOWN FINN would arrive on the same ferry on which Hester and Lily were leaving. Somehow, his timing had always been like this. I watched him make his way down the gangway in the crush, his bag over his shoulder, wondering whether I'd be able to see them off before he saw me.

"*Mum!*"

"Yes? What?"

"We're leaving! We're going! Do you even care? *Lily!*" she barked.

Lily was standing apart, sulking. Every now and then I saw her glance back toward the fence, and, yes, there was Yorgos slouching against it, smoking a cigarette. When Hester had retrieved her from the beach, I'd seen, for the first time, the flash of defiance in her eyes. And then, all the way back to the house she'd sat in front with me, maintaining a stubborn silence in the face of Hester's recriminations. And at last, when I'd said, "That's enough now, Hester," she'd flashed me such a look of gratitude that I wished I could turn the car around and take her right back to the beach.

"Lily!" Hester barked now.

But Lily was deaf to her.

"Darling," I whispered, "just let her be sad. Remember what it was like? It's awful."

Hester hung her head then, furiously wiping at her eyes. She'd always cried like this—furious, shuddering, biting her lips together.

"Darling," I said, "what if we go off for a weekend together after I return? Just you and me? Lily can go to Saul?" Perhaps, I was thinking, wresting my life so relentlessly for myself over all these years was what had left the structure of hers tilting like this.

"We could have done that here!" she said. "But, of course—"

"Hey!" said Finn, coming up and putting his hand on her shoulder. "You're not leaving, are you?"

She nodded. "That's our ferry."

"So, skip the ferry and stay on with us!"

Us? I turned aside, pretending to dig for something in my

bag. "Hey!" he said again, touching my shoulder this time. "Tell her to stay! Where's Lily?"

Hester snorted, drying her cheeks with the back of her hand. "We have to go," she said. "I've got summer school. And she has riding camp."

"Fuck summer school!" he said. "Fuck riding camp! Why're you wasting your life in a classroom anyway?"

The crowd began to surge forward.

"Lily!" Hester yelled. "Come on! Now! Bye, Mum!" She threw her arms around me, weeping again.

"Dumb, dumb," said Finn, watching them join the crowd.

Lily didn't turn, not even for a last look from the top of the gangway.

"Agh," Finn said, "what's the matter with them?" Then he beamed down at me, his Ray-Bans glinting in the sun. "And how're you, my little darling? Ready to say sorry?"

It was his favorite ploy, or joke, or perhaps he actually believed in the reversal. And really I was sorry—sorry for Hester, and for Lily, and wishing truly now that there were something I could do to make them happy.

I watched the ferry until it was out of sight, and then led the way to the car, thinking how ridiculous it was to have him back, and whether to drop him at the hostel.

"I'm not sure it was worth your while coming back," I said, starting the car. "Agnes and Wilfred are still here. She leaves tomorrow, but he'll torment Bess with his presence as long as it suits him to."

"That slimebag's nothing to me. Why would I give a damn about him?"

I shrugged.

"Listen, just stop this nonsense and marry me," he said.

"You know you want to tie the knot. Everyone knows it." He rolled down the window and hung his head out into the wind. "We could live here if you like," he shouted. "Although it might get a bit boring. But if that's what you want, okay."

"'Tie the knot'!" I laughed, I couldn't help it. His nonsense made me happy. It always had.

☉

Hester (finis)

I've just reread this journal, start to finish, and find I've learned nothing more than I knew already. Not that it hasn't been a fine antidote to the idiocy of So Long, *but, in their own way, the entries have been just as wrought, just as ordered into shape, just as far in their orderliness from the mess and disarray of life. All that writing this has brought me is a sort of sadness for things I can do nothing about. "It could bring to the relationship closure," Dania had said. Closure? I should have included that nonsense in my final screed for "à GG."*

So, what I'm thinking now is that I'll tear out these pages—there aren't that many—and rip them up. Then drop the pieces into the Aegean as we ferry away from this island. The trouble is that I've never much warmed to that sort of self-generated, self-conscious ritual, not even the scattering of ashes.

So, perhaps I won't tear them up. Perhaps, if I read them over when I'm seventy-five or eighty, I'll find the sadness has faded, like the color in the old photographs.

Or perhaps not.

◉

THEY WERE ALL AT THE house when we arrived, the French doors wide open, and Mohammed waddling in and out.

Finn stopped on the threshold. "I'll go to the room."

"What room?"

"Don't play games. I need a shower—" He peered out at the veranda. "Who's the movie actor?" he said. "In the chase long."

"Rex. And please don't do your 'chase long' number here, they won't find it funny."

"Fuck them, who's Rex?"

"Bess's sometime lover."

He snorted. He'd always snorted at the word "lover," although he was watching this one with keen interest. "Movie actor?" he said again.

I walked off to the kitchen and started to put things in order. We'd sent Gladdy on a trip to Naxos with her church ladies and it was a relief to have the kitchen back to myself.

"Oy," said Dania, coming in. "It's like Times Square here."

"I know, I know." I banged a few dishes around.

"And I am having again heat waves, can you believe it?" she said, flapping a dish towel. "After all these years! It's like being again forty."

"Daniushka," I whispered, "you didn't tell anyone else that you pushed her, did you?"

She shook her head.

"Good. But what about that recording? The one she made? Amos choking?" I looked hard at her. "What the hell possessed you, Daniushka?"

She shook her head, defeated for once. "Revenge is the end of nothing," she said.

❧

Ruth, dear, funny as it may be, we're going to have to pass on this one. After Bess's last one, which created a storm of e-mails (not necessarily a bad thing) we thought something more positive would be a nice way to end the year. The recipes went down a treat :) Have the children left? What about a column saying how you miss them? Or at least the grandchildren? Something bittersweet? Give it a think. I know you must be packing up crazily, but a penultimate one in Greece would be great. Then, for the last "à Go Go," something about being home again? Just reaching out :) Sxx

❧

REX WAS THERE WHEN FINN and I emerged from my room the next morning. He raised an eyebrow at me when Finn wasn't looking, and then stood, holding a hand out to Finn. They were perfectly matched, both tall, gray, and pleased with themselves.

"Are you still at the hostel?" I asked Rex.

"Oh no," said Rex, "thank God, no." He laughed. "I'm back at the hotel, at least until this afternoon."

"They've got room now?" I said. I couldn't imagine enduring another night of Finn's snoring. "Finn," I said, "you're going to the hotel tonight."

"We'll see about that." He put an arm around my shoulder.

"Ruth, listen," said Rex. "I'm going to need your help with something."

Finn's grip tightened.

"It's a long story," he said, "but, in short, we're leaving on the one o'clock ferry."

"'We'?"

"That's the point. Irina and I and the baby."

Finn whistled.

"What help?" I said, loosening myself from Finn's grip.

"Bess has a thing about Irina," he said. "I don't blame her, of course, all things considered."

"But, as I understand it, the child isn't even yours." Have you got your hands on Bess's bank account yet? I wanted to ask. Because, if you have, I'll call the authorities to stop you boarding the ferry.

"Whatever the case," he said brusquely, "I'm going to marry Irina and adopt Eugenia. That's what Irina called her. Lovely name, isn't it?"

"And Wilfred?" I said.

He smiled then, flashing teeth. "They've had enough of paternity, it seems. They're giving the other child back as well."

"They're *what*?"

"They say, of course, that the child will be better off, but they're the ones who'll be better off, any fool can see that. Well," he said, slapping his thigh and giving a quick glance at the stairs, "I've scribbled it all down here. Bess'll be okay, you know. I've never known anyone who lands on her feet the way she does. But you'll bolster her up a bit, won't you, Ruth?"

Finn and I sat in silence after the door closed, the muffled sound of Dania's voice filtering through as she conducted one of her morning sessions. After a while, Bess's door opened below, and I heard her step, her shuffle, her sigh as she began to haul herself upstairs.

"Let her have her breakfast first," Finn whispered. He adored presiding over a drama, and often I'd pretend to play along. Now, however, I stood up and put the envelope in her place at the table.

"Was that Rex I heard?" she said, coming in. "At this hour? Oh, Finn, hello. What's this?" she said, picking up the envelope.

"I'm playing Gladdy today," I said. "I'll make the coffee."

๏

Dear Stacey,

Alas, positive isn't going to work for the last two. Or ever. If I have any talent, it lies in the opposite direction. So when I'm confronted with the sort of positive thinking that pervades So Long, it makes me want to hang myself. Or, at least run off in search of someone as negative as I am about the sorts of things your readers are so positive about. If we were talking about joy here, real joy, or even ordinary happiness—those unexpected moments, or stretches of moments, that don't arrive on order—well, that's a gorgeous subject, a deep and complex subject that I don't think would be at home in a magazine like So Long.

So, why don't we just call it a day with "à GG?" I think we'd both feel rather liberated just to put it behind us, as you might say. Don't you?

With fond regards and thanks,
Ruth

๏

"DID *YOU* KNOW?" BESS SHOUTED at Agnes. "Did you know they're giving that Mustafa back?"

Agnes closed her eyes, doubtless to make being out of the moment easier. Her bags were lined up in the hall and I was driving them down to the ferry. "They're going this afternoon," she said. "By plane."

We'd been enduring Bess's outrage all morning. Clearly, Agnes knew as well as I did that it was Rex who was at the heart of it.

"They're giving him back because he'll be better off with his own kind of parents," said the girl, hitching herself yet again onto Agnes's lap.

"And who's putting that rot into your head?" Bess demanded. "Listen to me, my girl: They're giving him back because they can't stand him. A lot of parents can't stand their children. The difference is that they *can't* give them back because they're *theirs*. See?"

"You wouldn't give me back, would you, Mummy?" squeaked the girl, looking up into Agnes's face. She was getting on my nerves almost as much as she was getting on Bess's.

"Oh, for God's sake!" snapped Bess. "Don't start that nauseating duet again, please."

"When are we going, Mummy?" the girl said.

Bess banged her coffee cup back onto its saucer. "Why don't you go now?"

I looked at my watch. "Come," I said, "we can have a coffee down at the port while we wait for the ferry."

"Look," Bess said to Agnes, "I know I'm being a cow, but the girl's nine, for God's sake. You've got to set her free or she'll land up in a loony bin."

Agnes gave her mirthless laugh. "Oh, Ma!" she said, leaning over to kiss the top of her head. "Emma," she said, "Giles. Come and say goodbye to Grandmother, please."

As I drove them down to the port, chatting to Agnes about things that didn't matter, I was thinking of Lily and Eleftheria's Yorgos, and wishing, oh wishing, I'd listened to Finn and got her to stay on for another few days of happiness.

༺ට

Oh no, Ruth, dear, don't leave us in the lurch! What if we edit your
last piece down a bit, taking out some of the more flagrant red flags?
You should see the fan mail we get about you! Whisper-whisper:
Amy wants you to go on with the column after the year is up, but
keep that under wraps or she'll have my hide. Okay? Peace? By the
way, we'd love a column about those moments of happiness. Could
you work one in? Sxx

༺ට

Gripp Redux #1
When Stefan Gripp came to, he was stretched out like a dead man,
staring up into a moving kaleidoscope of light and dark. After a while,
he saw that it was the bough of a tree, and that a gentle rain was falling
through the canopy, fluttering the leaves. I must be on an outcropping,
he thought, looking around. But, with mist below and cloud above, it
was impossible to be sure. Slowly, inch by inch, he backed himself up
against the tree trunk. And only then did he run the usual check: arms,
legs, cash, notebook, revolver. All in place. O'Donohue must have been
in one hell of a hurry, he thought, or decided I was dead already.

༺ට

I MANAGED WITH DIFFICULTY TO get Finn down to the house
Hester and Agnes had just vacated. Doesn't make sense, he kept
muttering—he for whom making sense had never ranked very
high. The truth was, he was embarrassed. He was also wounded
that I hadn't warmed sufficiently to the gesture he'd made in
returning to endure his snoring and take him back into my heart
(as he'd have put it).

And yet, he was in my heart. If I'd been writing him into a

novel, I'd have pushed him upstage, at least until the final scene. But this wasn't a novel, and it was awkward having him back, out of the blue, only weeks before we were all due to leave anyway. It was awkward, too, with Dania, and with Bess mourning Rex, and with Gladdy clucking around like an enraged hen.

"Bess," I said, "you didn't pay Finn's airfare, did you?"

She stretched luxuriously. "I offered, but honestly, Ruth, he's a decent chap—he said no thanks. Don't be a cow. Just give him a chance."

"And Rex?" I said. "What happened to your offer there?"

"Oh, that bastard!"

"But, listen," I said, quite serious now. "Did he take the money? Did he, Bess?"

I watched her carefully, but she didn't flinch. "I didn't give him a chance," she said. "He had the gall to try, of course, but I'm quite good at sabotaging a subject before it can even come up."

I laughed. She was right. I'd seen her at it.

"Can't you just see them in a bedsit," she said. "Nappies and buckets and mops, and a scheme for making a killing on nipple cream—?" She broke into a peal of shrieking laughter.

"Wot's so funny?" said Dania, coming in from her morning's labors. "Where's Finn?"

"He'll be up soon," I said. "Did you change your ticket?"

"All changed, no penalty! Amn't I great?"

"Great, great, great," sang Bess, back at her laptop. "But look at this. Dania, come here! You'd be fabulous in this!"

Dania strolled over to the window seat and peered at Bess's screen. "What is it?" she said. "A blanket? Wot?"

"It's a cloak! See where the arms come through? And there're pockets."

"But orange? I don't wear orange."

"But it's the best sort of orange! The Italians do that orange. You'd be gorgeous in it."

Dania stood up straight. "How much for that blanket?"

"It's on marked-down markdown, and it's your birthday present. Where do you want them to send it?"

"No, no, no." Dania shook her head vigorously, accustomed only to the other side of generosity. "This is crazy," she said, "mark-down or markup."

"Consider it first prize for getting rid of Wendy. I'll get you the skirt to match if you get rid of Dinny's wife."

Dania laughed then, a real laugh and, for a few moments, we were all laughing together. It was as if we'd just arrived and had the whole year still ahead of us.

"What's the joke?" said Finn, coming in. "Come on, tell me!" He'd always adored women's laughter, and could never understand why it stopped when he tried to join in.

"How about that restaurant down on the water?" he said. "The one with octopuses hanging on a string outside?"

"Lots of them they have octopi henging," said Dania.

"He means Halaris," I said. "Anyone want to go?"

But we were a couple now, he and I, and so they pretended to have other things to do. Without them, however, it would feel out of step, sitting at Halaris, ordering calamari when what I really wanted was for the three of us to have these last weeks to ourselves—just us, for once.

☙

"WINE?" FINN SAID, AS SOON as we were seated at the restaurant. He grinned across the table at me, still enormously pleased with his gesture in returning. "Beer? Can't remember the name of the one I used to order."

"Mythos?"

"That's it! One half carafe white wine, one Mythos."

I stared at the boats on the water, thinking of Rex and the yacht coming into harbor. How long ago it seemed now. It also seemed simulated, heartless, and suddenly I was ashamed of it for that. I sipped my wine in silence.

"Hey," he said, "talk to me!"

"I'm not in the mood."

"You're not going to bring up what happened last time, are you? Because if you are, I'll leave right now." He stood up.

"So, leave! Who asked you to come back in the first place?"

"You want me to leave?" he said, leaning toward me.

"I want you to stop making a scene."

He turned to the table next to us. "She wants me to leave," he said, "so I'm going to stay." He sat down again.

I couldn't help it, I laughed.

"See? I made you laugh!"

"You make me wonder what the hell I'm doing with you."

"That's not what you were saying the other night."

"Oh, for God's sake, Finn, do grow up."

"Marry me and I'll grow up immediately. You won't believe the difference. Boom, an adult."

⊚

TWO POLICEMEN WERE WAITING AS we came through U.S. immigration. One stepped forward. "Dr. Dania Weiss?"

"Here I am," Dania said. "What's happened?"

Gladdy, Bess, and I stopped our luggage carts behind her.

"Move ahead, please," the policeman said to us. He was small-eyed, thick-faced, frightening.

"But look—" Bess said.

"Move ahead, please!" he said again.

And so we moved ahead, and out through customs, into the crowded lobby. Agnes was waiting and, at the back of the crowd, Finn as well, his arms opened wide. He'd returned a week earlier, and with his tan and his shirtsleeves rolled up, he looked ridiculously young for his age.

"They've taken Dania," I said.

"Who? Where?"

"Two policemen. We don't know where."

"Want me to phone O'Donohue?"

"Yes! Now!"

"Now? I'll do it tomorrow. Come on, let's get out of here."

But Gladdy pushed her cart into his path. "Mr. Finn," she said, "you phone your friend now."

"Ma," said Agnes, "what's going on?"

"Forget it," said Finn. "It's Sunday. He won't answer."

There was no point in arguing with him, that much I knew. And maybe, after all, Dania would talk her way out of a night in the police station. "Amn't I great?" she'd say. "They just took me under their wings."

Yael ran up, breathless. "Sorry I'm late!" she said. "Traffic! Where's my mother?"

☙

Gripp Redux #2

There are advantages in returning from the dead, Gripp thought. For one thing, no one expects you back. Still, he took the precaution of buying a straw hat and a pair of large sunglasses at a tourist shop. He also grew a neat Greek mustache.

And then, coming out of one of the Byzantine alleys at the port, he almost ran into O'Donohue. The man was red-eyed, unkempt, unshaven.

He's had a hard time of it, Gripp thought, searching those cliffs for my body.

He watched him shuffle past. Then he spun around and came up behind him, pressing the nose of the revolver into the small of his back. "Keep moving, O'Donohue," he said. "Hands away from your pockets."

A man like O'Donohue, thought Gripp, knows when his life is over.

EPILOGUE

HESTER MADE A THIRD MARRIAGE, this time to a childless widower much older than herself. She found him online, and hopes, I think, to inherit a comfortable life from him. They live—not very happily, says Lily—in Florida. I see her once or twice a year.

Lily, on the other hand, I see all the time. She is a doctor now. As soon as she finished her internship, she joined Doctors Without Borders, went off to Africa, and barely survived a severe case of cerebral meningitis. She lives with Sevan, an Armenian pediatrician, who is her lover. (Finn objects to the word "lover," of course, but that is what Sevan is, and I like him despite his unregenerate love of puns.) Lily herself has become the delight and comfort of my old age. Almost everything about her surprises me with happiness, including the informal competition she's now running among pediatricians for titles of children's books that will never be published. So far, she's awarded third prize to "You Were an Accident," second to "Daddy Drinks Because You Cry," and first to "You Are Different and That's Not Okay." She is still devoted to horses, and her kitchen is plastered with the ribbons she's won.

A year after we returned, Dania moved to Wisconsin because Yael had joined a practice there. And Noam soon followed with his family. Wisconsin, she reports, is the most wonderful place in the world, apart from Israel, and why don't I consider coming there myself? She herself never seems to consider that I have people in my own life—Lily, Finn, others—or that I might like being where I am.

As it happened, she did manage to talk herself out of a night in the police station our first day back. And despite the fact that she could not be forced by law to hand over her professional notes on Wendy, she did so voluntarily. In light of these, the recording Wendy made of their phone conversation was deemed inadmissible, and Wendy's death an accident. We were all called to give evidence, including Gladdy, and to this day I have Wendy on my conscience. The only punishment Dania received was a reprimand from the psychotherapy board for accepting gifts from a patient. She never returned to live in California, although she does visit every summer. "Ruthi," she says, "amn't I great? I have the best of all worlds!"

And, of course, I agree.

I never wrote another column for *So Long*, claiming Gripp as an excuse. But I did suggest Bess for the purpose, never thinking she'd agree. As it turned out, I was quite wrong. And then, after one or two "à Go Go's," she was offered an agony column by the local paper. And now "Ask Bess" is syndicated throughout the country. Clearly she has found what she wants, whether or not she has the word for it. Her specialty is fat women. And it's been getting raving reviews, as Dania would say, ever since.

Despite objections from the wellness industry, Bess now flies all over the country, rallying fat women everywhere. She's even started her own line of overpriced tents. "Not overpriced at all!" she says. "Have you seen the fabric? The cut? The seams?"

So I've stopped teasing her. In fact, I've come to adore her. We see each other several times a week when she's in town, and even when Finn joins us it's as if he's never been more to her than what he is now—an old darling who made the grand gesture of traveling halfway around the world to surprise me with his presence.

As for Wilfred, Bess sent him back his debit card—which, she reports, he didn't like at all. Bullies never like losing their hold over you, she says, especially if you're their mother. The fact is, she's now making her own little fortune, what with the column, the talks, the tents, and the book she's written. It's been sitting comfortably on the bestseller list for twenty-six weeks, much longer than my *Gripp Redux*, and shows no signs of dropping off. It's the title that's selling it, she says: *How to Make a Good Man a Better Lover; or, Unlocking the Secrets of the Universe for Fun & Profit.*

Meanwhile, she's spending as freely as ever. But not on Rex. He lasted about three months with Irina before taking off for the Bahamas again. No doubt, says Bess, he's hoping to find himself a widow there, or on one of the cruise ships that hire him to dance with their widows. That's where she found him again, on a ship she was taking through the Panama Canal with a group of her fat ladies. They had about ten days together, and that was quite enough, she said. Sayonara, Rex.

Gladdy still lives with her, of course. Quite soon she found a new church and a new set of friends. But when they started asking her to give a talk about herself—the world she'd left behind and why she'd left it—she turned them down flat. "Trouble-makers," she said. "They want to stir things up."

When Bess suggested a catering business for Gladdy and bought a little bakery around the corner, that was the start of Gladdy's new life. After some months, when the bakery began to catch on, Gladdy took on a helper, and then another. And every day now there are lines of people outside Gladness Bakery. Most popular is my grandmother's honey loaf, and also her Victoria sponge cupcakes with vanilla icing. Recently the morn-ing paper ran a two-page spread on Gladdy during Black History month. "But they make a big mistake!" Gladdy complained. "I am not American. And those others they are not African. That is the difference between us."

"She's damn right there," says Finn, slapping his thigh. He's come to love Gladdy almost as much as she's allowed herself to be fond of him. Often I hear her high-pitched trill of laughter when he's with her. But if I ask him what brought it on, he just says, "That's between Gladdy and me."

One day she said, "I am hope, Miss Ruthi, that you marry Mr. Finn."

And in the end that is exactly what I did. It hasn't made much difference. For what is such a marriage if not a gesture in itself? A sort of flourish in the face of the gods between two people who, despite themselves, have found each other again be-fore their lives have had a chance to run their natural course?

ACKNOWLEDGMENTS

FOR THE GIFT OF TIME, peace, and a beautiful place in which to write, I thank the Bogliasco Foundation, Civitella Ranieri, the Corporation of Yaddo, and the Spíti tis Logotexnias in Greece. Sarah Crichton's enthusiasm, humor, and brilliant counsel have kept me going. And to a lunch with Jennifer Rudolph Walsh—whirlwind of intelligence and energy—I owe this book. Thank you!